HUNTING THE LADY OF THE NIGHT

Novels by C. M. Wendelboe

BITTER WIND MYSTERIES
Hunting the Five Point Killer
Hunting the Saturday Night Strangler
Hunting the VA Slayer
Hunting the Mail Order Murderer
Hunting the Lady of the Night

SPIRIT ROAD MYSTERIES
Death Along the Spirit Road
Death Where the Bad Rocks Live
Death on the Greasy Grass
Death Etched in Stone
Death through Destiny's Door
Death Under the Deluge

TUCKER ASHLEY WESTERN ADVENTURES
Backed to the Wall
Seeking Justice
When the Gold Dust Died in Deadwood
Fork in the False Trail

NELSON LANE FRONTIER MYSTERIES
The Marshal and the Moonshiner
The Marshal and the Sinister Still
The Marshal and the Mystical Mountain
The Marshal and the Fatal Foreclosure

HUNTING THE LADY OF THE NIGHT

A BITTER WIND MYSTERY

C. M. Wendelboe

Encircle Publications

Farmington, Maine U.S.A.

Encircle editor: Cynthia Brackett-Vincent

Author photograph by Heather M. Wendelboe

Published by:

Encircle Publications
PO Box 187
Farmington, ME 04938

info@encirclepub.com
http://encirclepub.com

The lady shuffled into the night, her destiny foretold,

Plodding along into the dark, the blackness will unfold,

Thinking of the money ahead and of those she'd have to hold.

Fearing those she'd bed tonight, so heartless and very cold.

Recalling a man she once had, her thoughts turned to years before,

That man who had treated her like a lady, not like a common whore.

That man who had treated her decently, who had been so gentle and kind,

The man she'd always been searching for, but thought she'd never find.

Now, so close to her home, she would stop and take a look

At the child behind the door, that beauty from a picture book.

She turned the key and went inside, her heart beating fast,

As she looked down at the child and saw the man from her distant past.

The lady strode into the night, her destiny foretold

Holding her head so very high, her posture so very bold.

Thinking that with that child at home, the night was not so cold,

Believing that with her child at home, she never would grow old.

But the Lady of the Night grew no older than she was on that cold night…

1

Arn Anderson squirmed, trying to get his legs under the dash of the VW Bug. Small, foreign cars never seemed to fit him. "You must be hard-up for a story to go talk to this woman."

Ana Maria downshifted and steered around a cyclist crossing the busy Cheyenne street. "I have to dig up something interesting before DeAngelo sends me on another boring b.s. story."

Arn smiled at that, recalling Ana Maria coming home from the TV station right after her broadcast of a buffalo sale at the bison ranch south of town. She had complained all during supper to Arn and his live-in handyman/gourmet chef Danny that nothing interesting was coming her way.

Until this morning. She had picked up Arn for lunch mere moments after the murder in Denver came across the wire: Happ St. John was found strangled not a week after he had been interviewed about a decades-old homicide case in Denver, the murder of prostitute Josie Dexter. When the Denver CBS affiliate aired that the recent victim was questioned in the now-cold case, which had been reopened by the Metro Cold Case Division, Arn recognized the name. Unless there was another Happ living in the city, which he doubted.

After Arn was transferred to Metro Homicide from the Patrol Division when he worked at the Denver PD, the division commander dumped the Josie Dexter cold case on his desk to see if he could solve it. Just like the division commander did with all new detectives their first day on the job, and it remained unsolved. At the time, Arn had no more insights into it than what the other investigators had. Each new man to Robbery-Homicide who had examined the case of the prostitute found strangled to death and stuffed semi-nude in a dumpster, only pieces of her jeans remaining on her, uncovered nothing more than the previous detective had.

"Pretty coincidental that this St. John character is found strangled just days after being pulled in for another interview," Ana Maria said. "He must have had some knowledge of that hooker's murder."

"Not necessarily," Arn said. "As I recall when I went over all the original reports years ago when I was in Metro Homicide, Happ was one of nine other guys who had been the last known people to see Josie Dexter alive at a bachelor party she... performed at. Plus, there was speculation at the time that the father of her child had killed her. Possibly one of the men at the party."

"St. John didn't give up anything when he was interviewed?" Ana Maria asked as she topped the overpass over the railroad tracks.

"Nothing more than the others. Either he didn't know who killed Josie Dexter, or he was playing mute to protect the one who did. I thought perhaps the father of her little girl might have been her killer, but Josie never told anyone who her daughter's father was, and there was nothing recorded on the birth certificate."

Ana Maria winked and said, "You've got a pretty good memory for an old dude. It's amazing that you can remember cases that far back."

"Josie Dexter's case... haunted me for years," Arn said. "A prostitute devoted to her six-year-old daughter, who was left alone in the world when her mother was murdered. And me not being able to add anything toward solving the case. But it still doesn't explain why we're on the way to talk with the ex-wife of a *recent* Denver murder victim."

"The dead guy—Happ—his ex-wife might have some tidbit of information that I can at least slip in as a sidebar for tonight's broadcast," Ana Maria said. "Anything so DeAngelo doesn't send me to cover some other crappy story no one will watch."

She turned onto 5th Street and motored past the line of houses that were originally built to accommodate railroad workers. Now, most showed disrepair, some with owners who seemed to be trying to keep their houses as unpresentable as possible. Sheila St. John's house was somewhere between dilapidated and run-down. Ana Maria pulled to the curb in front of the one-story house in need of a new coat of paint and something to prop up the leaning chain link fence. "Looks like your house when you first moved in," she told Arn as she climbed out.

"And mine would *still* look like that if Danny hadn't worked his remodeling magic."

As they passed the broken lawn mower sitting beside the

mailbox that was listing to the starboard, Ana Maria whispered to Arn, "I forgot to mention it, but don't let it slip that you're a former cop. Sheila's been in and out of the hoosegow ever since I started doing the police briefings in the morning. And she's not particularly fond of the law. Even retired ones."

"Anything serious that landed her in jail?"

Ana Maria dug into her purse for her notebook. "Just petty crap. Shoplifting. Drunk in public. Last time she was caught going through cars at Walmart and stealing stuff to sell. Did a month in the county lockup then."

"She sounds like a model citizen. Do I need to go in armed?" Arn asked.

"Not to worry—she gets a little tipsy now and again but she's really not a bad soul. Watch out for the pruning shears," and Arn stepped over the rusty set lying in the tall weeds overtaking Sheila St. John's walkway.

Arn stepped over the shears and whispered to Ana Maria, "What makes you think she'll talk with you?"

And Maria winked. "'Cause I'll put on a grim, sad face as I tell her about her ex-husband. I'll ingratiate myself to her in her hour of mourning. She's bound to slip in some juicy tidbit I can use."

"That's cold."

"No," Ana Maria said, "that's keeping DeAngelo off my butt."

She sidestepped an overturned lawn chair that attempted to cover rotten floorboards on the porch and rapped on the door. The screen bounced and threatened to come off its hinges as an anemic-looking woman came to the door and peered at them. Even though the screen was dirty, Arn could see she held a cigarette attached to a silver holder as she said, "If you two are selling some bullshit insurance, I'm not buying," with selling coming out as *szzzelling* through badly-fitting dentures.

Ana Maria took out her TV station identification and showed it to the woman. "Maybe you don't remember me, but I was in the press box at your last trial."

The woman squinted and her nose pressed against the screen. "I did my time in the county, so what the hell ya want this time? And who's that big bastard with you?"

"Trainee," Ana Maria lied.

Sheila laughed. "At his age, you better get him trained up quick 'cause he don't have too many reporting years left." She erupted into a coughing fit before turning back to Ana Maria. "Like I asked, what d'you need with me now?"

Ana Maria sucked in a deep breath. Arn had given many death notices in his thirty years as a law officer, but Ana Maria hadn't and he knew this would be her first. "No easy way of telling you, but your ex-husband was found murdered in Denver this morning."

"Which ex?"

"Happ."

"Happ? Murdered?"

"'Fraid so."

Sheila tilted her head back and laughed hard enough to start another coughing fit that threatened to hack up a chunk of lung. When she regained her composure, she said, "Good riddance to him. The world will be a better place without him."

"May we come inside and talk with you about him?" Ara Maria asked.

Sheila replaced the butt of her cigarette with a fresh one and lit it before saying, "I got nothing to say about that fool."

She started closing the door when Ana Maria blurted out, "There's a stipend the TV station gives for information."

Sheila stopped and peered through the screen door again. "Money, you say, just for talking? How much?"

"Depending on your information. That'll be up to the station manager, DeAngelo Damos."

Sheila laughed again. "If it's up to that tightwad, there won't be much. But what the hell—come on inside and we'll reminisce about ol' Happ."

Sheila didn't wait for them but started through the kitchen into the living room.

Arn whispered to Ana Maria, "Since when does tight-assed DeAngelo ever shell out money for information?"

"If he doesn't send Sheila a few lucky bucks after our little talk," Ana Maria answered, "I will. Got your Black Flag handy?"

Arn didn't have insecticide, and he wished he'd have been forewarned. He'd been in worse places as a cop, though he just didn't remember when. The trashcan overflowed with empty Hungry Man boxes that competed with empty cans of Grain Belt. Arn had long since been able to guess where a person was from by the brand of beer they drank. That and Sheila's slight accent told Arn she was probably from Minnesota. Wisconsin, perhaps.

"Have a seat anywhere," Sheila said as she brushed newspaper from a torn tweed-covered sofa onto to the floor.

Sheila took a six-pack of beer from a paper sack beside her recliner and ripped one from the plastic. "Beer?"

"Not for me," Ana Maria said as she grinned, "but my trainee here's a beer-drinking fool."

Arn glared at Ana Maria even as Sheila handed him a warm can of Grain Belt. She knew this would be the first beer he had drunk since moving to Cheyenne. But if it helped loosen the old gal's tongue…

He popped the top and slurped the foam that seeped to the top of the can. "Don't get any better than this."

Sheila held her beer up in a toast. "To Happy St. John. The nastiest husband a woman could ever wish for."

Ana Maria picked out the cleanest spot on the sofa, one that was mostly devoid of stains, and grabbed her pen from behind her ear. "It appears that Happ was not the ideal husband. In what way?"

"Drinking," She looked at her beer can. "Always partying with a bunch of guys he hung around with." Sheila chugged her beer and eyed another can. Perhaps, Arn thought, Happ's death affected Sheila more than she let on and she felt the need to get drunk. "Believe it or not, I never touched a drop of booze until I divorced that A-hole. We were living in Denver at the time. Not upper middle class by any extent but doin' pretty good for being married for only a few years. Happ had a job loading trucks for FedEx. Working days. Then, like I said, he'd go out partying with a bunch of guys. Going to strip clubs. To bars. Lord knows where else."

"Do you remember their names?" Ana Maria asked.

Sheila gave in and grabbed another can of beer. "Never met them, but I would have liked to, just like I would have liked to get divorced sooner for the way he gallivanted around."

"You eventually had enough," Arn said as he choked down another swallow. It wasn't that the brand of beer was bad, it was because he didn't drink. Especially warm beer.

"There was that *one* night when Happ went too far. He came home super late in the morning, damn near time to get up and go to work. His hand was bleeding something fierce. He said he cut it on a beer bottle in the bar. I knew he might just be telling me the truth, as he got into bar fights now and again. Happ always had that little-man attitude like he thought he could rumble with the big fellas. He refused to go to the emergency room to have it treated. 'Just wrap the thing in some gauze and I'll be okay.' So I did."

"And that's when you'd finally had enough?" Ana Maria asked. "When his hand was cut and bleeding from a night out with the boys?"

Sheila set her beer down and looked off into the corner as if the answer were there. After a long pause, she said, "No. The final straw was when I was wrapping his hand. I saw a fresh hickey on his neck and lipstick smeared on his collar. That's when I suspected he was cheating on me. So I gave him the bum's rush a week later. When he moved out, he was even going to take our computer with him until I called the cops for a civil standby to make sure I was safe while he was moving his shit out. He had to leave the 'puter."

She took another sip and smiled when she said, "After he left and I was alone, I started digging into his history on the 'puter. That was before DNA was discovered and I saw that the A-hole was researching how the police matched up blood types with suspects in crimes."

"Back then," Arn said, "blood type was useful only with a known suspect."

"But ol' Happ St. John had O-negative blood," Sheila said. "Rare."

"Blood banks yearn for O-type," Arn said. "Folks of any blood type can take O-negative."

Ana Maria leaned forward and laid her hand on Sheila's shoulder. "Is there any reason you can think of that anyone would have wanted to kill Happ?"

Sheila looked into the corner once again for her answer. "His annuity." She polished off her beer and tossed it into a paper sack beside her chair. "Those three peckerwoods he hung with invested in some foolproof… scheme. One I couldn't touch in the divorce. He was supposed to get a monthly check when the annuity reached maturity." She counted on her hand. "He was due to start getting checks in the next few years. Good luck finding out anything about that."

2

Danny dusted the French toast with confectioners' sugar before setting a plate in front of Arn and Ana Maria. "I'd like to go with you two to scenic Denver, but I need to shoot texture on that spare room."

Since he had caught the little, old Lakota squatting in Arn's mother's house, he and Danny reached an agreement: Danny would remodel the house in exchange for room and board. But he had done so much more. When Arn initially moved back into his mother's house, it was a mess after years of neglect. Danny had claimed he had an engineering degree and was capable of renovating the entire house, which it sorely needed. When Arn had asked him why he was homeless, Danny shrugged and said he had just dropped out of society.

Arn would later learn that the old Indian was on the lam for bombing an empty building with two others in Minneapolis involved in the American Indian Movement. Arn dug into it and learned the warrant had been purged years ago along with other old warrants that the statute of limitations had run out on. The investigators never caught Danny and the two other

AIM members, figuring they were dead by now anyway.

Arn had debated at the time whether or not to tell Danny what he had learned, fearing that he would light out of Cheyenne, leaving Arn to figure out how to remodel the house. But he eventually told Danny, and the old man decided to stay. He continued to work on the house and making—for all intents and purposes—gourmet meals for Arn and Ana Maria every night and many mornings, causing Arn to wonder what else the old man knew how to do.

"You guys gonna go see that hokey diving show at Casa Bonita while you're down there?" Danny asked.

"We might," Ana Maria answered. "Or we might save that for when we all three can have a night out. Ready?"

Arn finished his French toast and grabbed coffee in a Thermos before following Ana Maria out the door. She started for her VW when Arn said, "We're taking my Oldsmobile. I am not going to ride that far crammed into your Bug."

"But it gets a whole lot better mileage than your 442."

"That may be," Arn said, "but it's worth the trade-off not to have to fold and unfold myself every time I get in and out."

Arn stopped at a service station on the way out—the Olds never met a gas station it didn't like—before heading to Denver. Ana Maria wanted to interview the investigator working on Happ St. John's homicide, and DeAngelo had allowed her the trip. She had guilt-tripped Arn into coming along. "After all," she'd argued, "you are retired. Not like you got anything lined up for today, right?"

Arn didn't. Since returning to Cheyenne, he had taken on some private investigations and had even spent nights in rancher's fields watching for rustlers. But Ana Maria was right— he had nothing going on. Except helping Danny work on the house. But Danny always complained that Arn was inept in the handyman department and his work usually took the scrawny Indian more time to go back and correct what Arn had done. "Who's the Metro investigator handling the case?"

"Sal Bass," Ana Maria answered.

Arn groaned.

"Know him?"

"Unfortunately," Arn said as he pulled onto Interstate 25 heading south. "We call Sal Bass 'Sal the Ass' 'cause he was always, well, an ass. Thought he was God's gift to investigators. Horned in on everyone's cases like he was some great Sherlock Holmes. He should have retired by now, too, but when I was there, he was paying alimony to his first three wives and needed to stay on the job."

Their ride to Denver was uneventful and their conversation more so, touching on such subjects as the community events that Ana Maria had to cover, events that did nothing to spur her curiosity. When she worked at the CBS affiliate in Denver about the time Arn met her, she was fairly giddy at the crime stories she was sent to cover. She had developed an insouciance concerning mundane stories. And like cops who might not admit it, dead bodies and the stories they held were far more interesting for her.

"I doubt Sal will give you any pearls of information about Happ's murder."

"I disagree," Ana Maria said. "When I called him to set up an interview, the first thing he asked was if I would identify him on my broadcast. When I took the middle road and said perhaps, he said he welcomed any exposure at this point in his career."

"And I bet the second thing he asked is if you're married."

"Sounds like you *do* know Sal Bass well. Is he some wolf I ought to be cautious around?"

Arn chuckled. "Like I said, he's got three ex-wives and looking for a fourth. Maybe moreso now, as it's been some years since I spoke with him. But for God's sake, the man is my age. If he chases you, run around the desk a few times. He's bound to pass out or have the big MI."

They pulled to the curb in front of Robbery-Homicide and walked into the building. The receptionist eyed them suspiciously until Ana Maria said she had an appointment with Detective Bass.

After several minutes, they were buzzed through the security door. "I know the way from here," Arn said, but an officer in a blue blazer emerged from a side room. "I'll escort you," she said. "Can't have people wandering the building."

She led Arn and Ana Maria down the hallway where he banged on a door with Sal's name on it. Sal opened it, his smile fading when he saw Arn. "Thought the little lady would be coming alone. Didn't figure on some old washed-up detective being with her."

"Maybe you ought to wash up a little yourself," Arn said. "Being in the police business at your advanced age can be deadly to the health and hygiene."

"You think I ought to retire? I'm as sharp as ever. Hell, I've aged quite well, don'tcha think?"

Arn eyed him, noting how Sal must have joined the Botox-of-the-Month Club, the crows' feet at the corners of his eyes gone. The sagging jowls and double chin that must have been lopped off by some incredibly skilled plastic surgeon. "That tanning machine must have cost you a bundle," Arn said, "beside the visit to the make-me-look-young doctors."

Sal just scowled at Arn as he motioned them into his office and to chairs arranged in front of his desk. He ignored Arn and turned to Ana Maria, looking her up and down. He tugged at the lapel of his tailored sharkskin and wool suit for a moment before saying, "You were a little cryptic as to just what you wanted to know about Happ St. John."

Ana Maria told Bass what Sheila had told him. "I need some information to fill in a broadcast that you will be mentioned in as the lead investigator."

Arn was sure he saw her bat her eyes when she asked, "Do you have any clues as to the murderer?"

Sal shrugged and tugged at one corner of his toupee. "I can tell you that ol' Happy didn't have much to say, hanging there with that sheet around his neck. He didn't even have the decency to leave a note."

"So, you do feel it was suicide like it was reported?" Ana Maria asked.

"One-hundred percent sure."

"Did he have problems recently that would cause him to want to hang himself?" Arn asked.

Sal glared at Arn as if he were an intruder into his flirting session with Ana Maria.

Sal leaned his elbows on the desk and said, "Look, I know

a homicide would be more dramatic for your broadcast, but it was suicide. Trust me. He had just been interviewed in that homicide the cold case detectives recently reopened… the murder of that streetwalker damn near thirty years ago. That Josie Dexter." Sal turned to Arn. "You know, the case you couldn't crack."

"And neither could you," Arn said. "None of us could. Did you talk with the cold case detective?"

"Why the hell should I? This is an open-and-shut suicide. Doesn't much matter what Happ told anyone else. He was DRT—Dead Right There—hanging from that bedsheet."

Ana Maria asked, "Can I have the spelling of your name so I get it right for my broadcast?"

"Sal Bass," he answered with a smile. "Like the fish."

Or the ass, Arn thought.

"Could you tell me," Ana Maria seemed to *coo*, "which detective is assigned Josie Dexter's case?"

"Roger Heinz," Sal answered. "Pretty young. Must have done something to piss off the brass to be assigned to Cold Case. But don't tell him I sent you 'cause he don't like me much for some reason."

"I can't imagine why," Arn said under his breath as he led Ana Maria out of the office.

When they had walked out of earshot, she said, "Makes me want to get my hand sanitizer out and wash my whole body. I think if you hadn't been there, good ol' Sal would have gotten a whole lot… friendlier."

Arn winked. "I told you, Sal's on the prowl for wife number four. Maybe you could fill that role."

"And like you said before, the man is *your* age." She nudged Arn, then asked, "What did Sal mean when he said you couldn't solve a case of a murdered prostitute? I thought you solved all your cases when you were in Metro."

"All except that of Josie Dexter," Arn began. "She was a streetwalker who was murdered a few years before I was transferred to Robbery-Homicide. Every new investigator got the Dexter case their first day on the job and allowed a week to solve it."

"But you didn't?"

Arn shook his head. "I didn't. Just like every other detective couldn't solve it. And it appears as if it's *still* unsolved." Arn had caught the Denver broadcast a few days ago where Josie's case had been reopened. "Let's hope they have more luck with some of the technology they have nowadays."

Ana Maria took her phone and started punching numbers. "With any luck, Roger Heinz is in today. Like you, I don't believe in coincidences. Happ St. John hanging himself so close to the Josie Dexter case being reopened *is* a little suspicious."

3

In comparison to Sal "The Ass" Bass, the cold case detective assigned to Josie Dexter's murder, Roger Heinz, seemed almost shy. Half Sal's age and dressed in a simple off-the-shelf suit, he acted impressed that anyone outside the police department would be interested in what he had to say. "I don't know what you want to know, but I will tell you if it's something I'm allowed to." He held the door to the dank, basement office for them and moved chairs so that they were closer to his.

Detective Heinz sat and said to Arn, "Ana Maria didn't mention *the* Arn Anderson would accompany her."

"Do I know you?" Arn asked.

Detective Heinz shook his. "But I know you—at least, I know of your reputation when you were in Homicide. Solved every case handed to you."

"Except Josie Dexter's."

"And you joined a long list of investigators who didn't. Perrier?"

Arn shook his head, but Ana Maria accepted a bottle. She uncapped it and paused before saying, "Tell us what Happ St.

17

John said when you recently brought him in for an interview on the Dexter case."

Detective Heinz stared at his bottle cap for a long moment. "I don't need to tell you that case is a luncher." He forced a laugh. "We definitely ate our lunch on that these many years. I'm still trying, though, and brought in Happ St. John, who was just one of six men still living who were the last to see Josie Dexter alive."

"As I recall from the old reports," Arn said, "the original detective brought in ten men for questioning who last saw Josie at a bachelor party."

"But there's only six left alive." Heinz rubbed his temples. "I'm afraid I pushed Happ St. John too hard in the interview, and look what happened—he hung himself."

"Wasn't your fault," Arn said. "Your job was to get to the truth. I would bet the others you questioned didn't hang themselves."

Detective Heinz laughed nervously. "The others I didn't squeeze like I did Happ. I felt he was close to breaking down. So I told myself after the interview that I'd wait for a week and let his conscience work on him before bringing him back in. Guess I should have brought him in sooner."

"Why did you pressure him and not the others?" Ana Maria asked.

Heinz put the cap back on his bottle without touching the water. "He became more fidgety the more I talked about Josie Dexter's murder. Especially when I asked if he had any knowledge of her body being tossed in a dumpster in Commerce City."

"Do you think he had information he was keeping to himself all these years?" Arn asked.

"I don't know," Heinz answered. "I just don't know. But there was something about his body language… the tone of his voice, that I suspected he knew more, and I pressed him. I should have reinterviewed him sooner before he went and offed himself."

Arn rubbed his own temple, trying to think back to the reports he had poured over that first day as a junior detective and for some weeks afterward before he gave up like everyone else had. "As I recall, the original detective thought Happ was especially nervous at the original interrogation, too."

"Neal Barton. He was gone by the time I started in Robbery-Homicide, but by what others said, he was a pretty thorough detective." Heinz stood and walked to a picture on the wall of a younger Roger Heinz in a white naval uniform and he straightened it. "His notes said that Happ St. John *was* nervous in the interview. But then he speculated every other married man he interviewed would be nervous lest their wives found out a stripper and streetwalker had worked the bachelor party they attended.

"Detective Barton made a note that Happ was trembling, but figured the little guy just couldn't take the cold. Came into the interview wearing a thick coat and gloves. Figured it was normal. October in the Rockies can get mighty cold at times, but I'm not telling you anything you don't already know."

"I wouldn't beat yourself up over Happ's suicide," Arn said. "It was his choice, for whatever reason he had."

"Damn it, I wanted to solve this cold case so bad… excuse the language, Ms. Villarreal."

"Ana Maria. And I've heard worse."

"But what I said is true," Detective Heinz said. "I worked my tail off trying to find something that would lead me to Josie

Dexter's killer. I even went to Cheyenne to interview one of the guys who was at that bachelor party. Gene Woods."

"Know him?" Ana Maria asked Arn.

"He's a master mason. He has his own brick business in Cheyenne. Specializes in decorative projects for the home. He's so good that he's booked up solid. That's according to Danny, who is no slouch when it comes to laying brick himself. But I take it Gene didn't remember anything new either?"

"He did not," Heinz answered. "All he could recall is what he told Detective Barton originally—that after Josie Dexter was done working the bachelor party, she left, saying she was going to hit the street where she could make some real money."

"By any chance, did Happ leave behind any relatives here in the Metro region?" Ana Maria asked.

"You'll have to ask Detective Bass, as that's his case."

"Roger," Arn said, leaning closer, "would you even want us to go back and talk with The Ass, as unpleasant as he is? Maybe you could just… take a quick peek in your computer at Happ's case and see if he left anyone on this side of the grass."

"I see your point," Heinz said before swirling his chair around to face his computer. His fingers did their keyboard magic and within seconds he said, "Looks like Happ was living with a cousin." He jotted the address down and handed Arn the slip of paper. "But don't tell Detective Bass I helped you, or he'll have my shield."

*   *   *

Marcella Bates lived in a two-bedroom home off of 72nd Ave.

that was nearly as dilapidated as Sheila St. John's house. But where Sheila made no effort to improve the looks of her home, Marcella had done what she could to make it presentable. A coat of lime-green paint had recently been applied—probably a give-away from some paint store because few people painted their houses florescent green. The yard bore little grass, like Sheila's, but Marcella kept the weeds cut close to the ground. A picket fence half-way around the yard leaned a little but hadn't fallen down yet.

Ana Maria stepped onto a narrow porch that sported two new pieces of wood to replace rotten ones and rapped on the door. A squat woman in a paisley dress held a white handkerchief as she dabbed at tears on her cheek. She looked at Ana Maria then to Arn and said, "The police again. I have told you people all I know—"

"We're not police." Ana Maria showed the woman her press credentials. "We would like to talk with you about your cousin, Happ St. John."

The woman hesitated for a moment before she unlocked the screen door. "If it will let the world know what a lovely man Happ was… come in."

She stepped aside to let Ana Maria and Arn into a small kitchen, made smaller by the two-burner stove and apartment-sized refrigerator in one corner. The Formica countertop was chipped but clean, and a slightly dented trash can was neatly stashed in one corner.

Marcella led them past a bathroom that looked almost too small to use and to her living room. Two chairs with TV trays beside them, the only furniture in the room, were parked in front of a small screen television. She motioned to one of the chairs and said, "Please set in Happ's chair. I don't have any others—"

"That's all right," Arn said. "I need to stand and stretch anyway."

Marcella turned her chair so that it nearly faced Ana Maria. "What is it you wish to know?"

"Tell us about your cousin," Ana Maria began in that soothing tone she often used when she wanted people to open up to her. Arn expected Marcella to detail what a party animal Happ was, recalling what Sheila said about her ex-husband.

Instead she said, "Happ St. John was the most loving, kind man anyone could want around. You broadcast *that*."

Ana Maria, like Arn, had learned long ago in her career that if one just remains silent, the person being interviewed will open up. Marcella did.

"Happ wasn't very handy around the house, but he did the best he could to fix things whenever they broke. He often said he wanted to stay busy to stay sober. Never bought anything for himself. Gave me a small amount every time he got that small annuity every quarter. The only places he went were AA meetings and the Cornerstone Mission to help serve the evening meals. Singing for his supper like a lot of the homeless folks who stopped in off the street." She chuckled as if recalling fond memories. "Happ even did the preaching a time or two when the Mission sky pilot was indisposed with his favorite libation and didn't show for the preaching."

Arn tried to square Happ's description as the womanizing, party animal of years past that Sheila described with what Marcella just told them. "I have to be honest, Happ St. John's name came up in police reports more than a few times, but you said he preached at the Cornerstone Mission. Who do *you* think would want him murdered?" Arn asked, recalling the many times he had asked survivors just that, knowing the answer might rest close to home.

Marcella wrung the handkerchief as if it were soaked with tears. "Nobody. Happ completely turned his life around about thirty years ago. He quit drinking and doing dope when he got fired from his job at the warehouse, and he came to me a broken man. It was the lowest point in his life. He found Jesus and was a different man from then on. Material things meant nothing to him, and he was content to live off that small quarterly annuity and pick up day jobs now and again. Sell blood every month for a few dollars that he'd give to me for groceries."

Marcella stood and arched her back. "As to who would want him dead... Happ had some words with a couple fellers who'd stop by the mission now and again. But Happ... he always turned the other cheek. Just like the Good Book says to do. But I already told the police all this. They said they need to keep Happ's body in cold storage until a supervisor can clear it, but I would like his body released to me for burial."

Marcella paced in front of the TV trays before stopping and asking Ana Maria, "Could *you* ask the detectives if they can release Happ's body for burial? Even though Happ didn't kill himself—"

"Detective Bass assured us that Happ hung himself after being questioned about a decade-old homicide."

"Makes no difference what the detective thinks," Marcella said. "Happ would never kill himself, no matter what."

"What makes you so sure?" Ana Maria asked.

"God. Happ said now and again that the Lord gave him his life and it was up to Him when He wanted to take it back. Under no circumstances would he have hung himself."

"Did you tell that to Detective Bass?" Arn asked.

Marcella guffawed. "That man didn't want to hear anything I said. I tried to tell him about Happ's faith, but he never even acknowledged me."

4

"You sure DeAngelo is going to approve the room?"

Ana Maria unlocked the motel room door. "He'll bitch, but I used the company credit card, so it'll be a month before the bill comes due and he realizes the expense. By then, I'll have an in-depth story for my nightly broadcast that'll more than pay for this room."

When they entered the room, Ana Maria peeled off and into the bathroom while Arn claimed the bed closest to the door. He unwrapped his new off-brand jeans and shirt and laid his tighty-whities beside them. They hadn't planned on staying overnight in Denver and hadn't packed back at the house, forcing them to make a quick stop to pick up some inexpensive clothes. Ana Maria insisted they follow up with Sal Bass regarding the information that Marcella told them. An overnight stay was better than driving back to Cheyenne only to turn around the next morning and drive back to fight Denver's morning traffic.

When Ana Maria finished in the bathroom and emerged in night clothes two sizes too big because they were on sale, Arn fought back a smirk as he went in. He laid the complimentary toothbrush and razor the motel clerk had given him beside the sink and changed into sweatpants and a shirt that were at least the requisite two sizes too large. When he finished, he came out of the room to find Ana Maria with pillows propping her up as she flipped pages in her notebook.

"What Marcella said is more than a little disturbing," Ana Maria said. "If what she said is true—and there's no reason to assume it's not—then Happ St. John's death wasn't suicide."

"That's what we have to convince The Ass of tomorrow."

"Why do you think Detective Bass was so quick to rule it a suicide?"

"Convenience," Arn answered as he fidgeted with the TV remote. "It makes his case load a lot easier if it's ruled a suicide rather than a homicide. That Happ was a helper at the Cornerstone Mission and a former drunk with a rap sheet for minor offenses I am sure turned Sal off on spending a lot of time on the case. If Happ had been a prominent citizen with a dozen relatives hounding Sal, things might be different. But the only person he has to fend off is Marcella."

Ana Maria grabbed the remote from Arn and worked some magic until the television powered on. "Find a movie," he said. "A comedy. Something to make me smile, 'cause when we talk with The Ass again in the morning, I won't be smiling."

* * *

Sal sat in his chair, a smug look on his face, sipping out of a stained coffee cup in the shape of Mickey Mouse. "I don't think I'm going to have Happ St. John re-examined by the ME, even with Marcella Bates bitching. She's been calling up here every day since Happ offed himself in back of the Cornerstone Mission, insisting he didn't hang himself."

"Sal," Arn said slowly, choosing his words carefully, lest he lose his temper, jump over the desk, and throttle The Ass, "I am sure Happ is still in the morgue awaiting release before the Medical Examiner submits her final report. Would it hurt any to ask the ME to look at Happ's injuries one last time?"

"Once again," Sal said, "there is nothing to indicate that his death was anything *but* suicide."

"Detective Bass," Ana Maria said softly, but Arn saw the look in her eye that told him she was becoming frustrated, too, "*I* would like Happ St. John's injuries looked at. From what Marcella Bates said, Happ would never kill himself."

"What the hell is this, bad cop, bad reporter routine? Get the hell out of my office. I got other cases to look at."

"We'll go," Ana Maria said with a stern voice, "and if you tune into my Cheyenne broadcast tomorrow, you will hear your name. More than once, I am certain."

"Hear my name in what context?" Sal asked.

"As the investigator in charge of a homicide, passing it off as suicide."

Sal stood abruptly and started around his desk when Arn stepped toward him. Sal backed off and said, "She can't slander me like that."

"It's only slander if it's not true," Arn said.

"But this is my case—"

"By the time the mayor and police chief hear your name and call me with follow-up questions about Happ's murder," Ana

Maria said, "you won't just be out of investigations but you'll be out of the department as well. Did I mention the police chief and the mayor regularly listen to my broadcasts?"

"You son-of-a—"

"Watch it!" Arn said.

Sal sat back in his chair and rubbed his forehead. "All right. I'll call the ME. Request another examination of Happ—"

"And I want one of us to attend," Ana Maria said. "Not that I don't trust you or anything."

Sal looked at Ana Maria and a wide smile replaced his worried look. "You'll just love to see an autopsy, sweet cheeks."

"I won't be the one sitting in on the re-examination," Ana Maria said, her own smile telling Arn she was pleased to have won this exchange with The Ass. "Arn is. I'm going to talk with Mrs. Brown."

"Who?"

"Just someone who might have seen Happ another time thirty years ago."

*   *   *

Arn stood beside Sal Bass on one side of the porcelain examination table, the Medical Examiner on the other side. "Your request sounded as if you had new information about the deceased," she said.

"*Someone* believes that Happ here didn't hang himself," Sal said, glaring sideways at Arn. Sal wasn't used to being put in his place like Ana Maria had done a few hours ago, and he still seethed. "I am in agreement with your original opinion that

Happ's death was *self*-inflicted," he told the Medical Examiner.

"Doctor McWilliams," Arn began, "in all my years as a lawman, I've only investigated two deaths whereby the victims hung themselves with sheets, and both had been inmates at the Detention Center. So, Happy hanging himself with a sheet sets off alarm bells with me."

"Fair enough," McWilliams said and brought an overhead lamp closer to examine Happ's neck. "Just like at the original autopsy, sheet marks—ligature marks on the victim's neck—are still visible."

Arn donned his glasses and squatted to get a better angle on… "What do you make of that round indentation?"

The ME followed Arn's finger and bent to the body, bringing the lamp closer. "I'll be damned. It's so faint, I did miss it at autopsy. What do *you* make of it?" she asked Arn.

Arn stood and stretched. "Tell me, was the hyoid bone broken or intact?"

"Intact," the ME answered. "But in some cases of hanging by suicide, it's not. What are you thinking?"

"That's pretty conclusive, I'd say," Sal said, gowned-up and wearing a face mask for the autopsy.

"Sal, turn around," Arn said.

"What—"

"Just turn around. I'm not going to hurt you."

"I don't know what you're about to do, but it better not mess up my suit."

Arn drew Sal close and slipped his arm around Sal's neck. Arn grabbed his choking hand with the other as if to increase pressure but stopped short. "What I'm thinking is that someone strong enough slipped up behind Sal, wrapped their arm around his neck, and choked him to death, then staged the scene to make it look like a suicide."

Sal broke away and straightened his suit. "That's just wild speculation on your part."

"Is it?" Arn said and turned to the pathologist. "Was his windpipe crushed?"

McWilliams shook her head for a moment before saying, "It was not, and it should have if he were hanging."

"And that small, round discoloration... look at my sleeve. I have a button on my coat sleeve. My guess is that discoloration is the result of someone's button on their choking arm contacting the victim's neck at the time of death."

Sal forced a laugh. "What, now—you think you can get the bruising enhanced to see the button mark better, maybe go about checking people's buttons? You're as nuts as you were when you worked Metro."

"No," Arn said. "The bruise is not that distinct. But it does add to the fact that Happ here was strangled from behind, and that he didn't hang himself."

"I concur," Doctor McWilliams said at last. "I will have to modify the death certificate."

Sal groaned. "Great. One more case I have to treat as a homicide."

"Welcome to Robbery-Homicide, hot shot," Arn said.

5

A rn watched the "cliff divers" at Casa Bonita restaurant, two young kids diving from a faux cliff into a pool of water ten feet below them. This had been sort of a goofy attraction since the restaurant opened, yet every time Arn was in the area, he stopped by for delicious authentic Mexican food and the entertainment. "What made you think I should talk with Mrs. Brown?" Ana Maria asked. "One of your gut feelings?"

Arn reached across the table and wiped a smudge of melted cheese from Ana Maria's cheek. "No, but I went over the report of Happ's 'suicide,' now ruled a homicide. When I saw that hand of his, he had a scar. Old, yet distinct. Deep at one time, and I got to thinking back to what Sheila said about her ex-husband, coming home late one night, hand cut open from a beer bottle. Remember, she wasn't positive about the date, but it would have been the night of—or a week give or take—of Josie Dexter's murder."

Ana Maria snapped her fingers. "The witness said she saw two men dump Josie's body into that dumpster and that one of the men had cut himself on the metal lid."

31

"Don't forget Happ was unusually nervous that first interview the original investigator conducted. And his officer notes said that Happ got even more so when pressed about Josie's murder."

"But *all* the men were nervous at their interviews," Ana Maria said. "At least the original detective thought it strange enough to make a special note of it. But like you said, all the men at that bachelor party were married. They'd understandably be anxious that their wives would find out."

"So we're back to who might want Happ dead? I'm betting someone from that party thirty years ago. After all, it was only a week after the Cold Case Division announced they were reopening Josie Dexter's case that Happ was killed."

A diver belly-flopped into the pool, sending sheets of water upward, some landing on their table, and Ana Maria wiped it away with her shirt sleeve.

"Did Mrs. Brown say anything else that might help?" Arn asked.

"I'm not sure at this point. She said Josie would go out working the streets or some private party and, because she lived next door, would ask Mrs. Brown to check in on Josie's daughter until she got home. Seems like the walls between their apartments were paper-thin. Mrs. Brown said she could hear most anything that went on in Josie's apartment, so she would know if the little girl was all right. And she emphasized that Josie never brought any johns to her apartment. That was sacred to Josie, never wanting to risk her little girl getting hurt."

"What happened to the girl after Josie was killed?"

"Mrs. Brown lost track of her. You going to eat the rest of those refried beans?"

"At my age, I don't handle beans so good." He slid his plate across the table, and Ana Maria scooped the beans onto her plate. "Family Services came and took the little girl. Mrs. Brown heard she was adopted out, but she doesn't know more than that about the child."

They finished their meal and made it to their appointment with Detective Heinz with an hour to spare. When he ushered him into his office and closed the door, he said, "What is this new lead you have on the Josie Dexter homicide?"

Ana Maria explained what she found out about Josie and her daughter from Mrs. Brown. When she finished, she sat looking at a silent Detective Heinz chewing on the end of his pen.

After a long pause, he dropped his pen and grabbed a manila folder on his desk. "This," he held up the file, "is a damn shame."

"How's that?" Ana Maria asked.

"This," he said again. "These few and brief interviews are all that was done to find Josie Dexter's killer at the time. Arn, you've worked homicides before… think how thick those case files grew."

Arn nodded knowingly. "After working the murders, my case files needed a banker's box to hold all of the paperwork."

"That's just my point." Heinz sat back and once more picked up his pen and began gnawing on it. "Josie's murder warranted more investigating than *this*. Just because she was a streetwalker and not a prominent citizen or one with influential connections didn't mean her death wasn't important. The investigating officer at the time talked to just a few people and wrapped it up. Went on to the next case that might involve a victim of some renown. Josie Dexter deserved better."

Arn studied Detective Heinz, visibly upset as he looked at Josie's thin case file. Metro had assigned Roger Heinz to cold cases, Arn was sure, because he cared *too* much for murder victims. Cared enough to keep digging and find their killers. Like he was doing now.

"I think Happ St. John was one of the men who dumped Josie's body into that dumpster," Arn said. "He might have been Josie's murderer."

"I'm listening."

"Happ had an old scar on his hand. His ex-wife said he came home from a night of partying with his hand ripped open. Bleeding all over the floor. Was blood noted on the dumpster?"

"By God..." Detective Heinz shuffled through the papers and came away with a thin packet marked EVIDENCE. He leafed through the packet and removed one sheet, which he dropped on the desktop. "I thought the evidence tech noted quite a bit of blood on the side of the dumpster." He flipped a page. "O negative."

"Happ was O negative," Ana Maria said. "Rare. Marcella said he gave blood at the blood bank once a month."

"That was something Detective Bass should have mentioned," Arn said. "If you guys met and went over cases more often—"

"With him?" Heinz said. "Sal Bass figures no one can add anything to what he already did on his investigations."

"This would be a good case for DNA," Arn said. "Happ's blood sample is begging to be compared with the blood on the dumpster."

"Good luck with that. We've been using Parabon Nanolabs out of Huntington, Virginia, and it takes a while for results to come back. That's if you want double validation."

"You mean corroboration with your own state lab?" Arn asked.

Heinz nodded. "To be admissible in court, the initial results have to be validated with an independent lab—"

"How about giving it to the state lab just to see if the blood on the dumpster and Happ's share the same DNA? Not for court but… just to satisfy an astute cold case detective?"

"I'll do what I can," Heinz said at last.

"That's if Metro still has the blood sample from the dumpster," Ana Maria said.

"If the sample was taken and entered into evidence," Heinz said, "we would still have it. We never destroy anything connected with a murder or even a suspicious death."

"In the meantime, maybe you could take Happ's photo to the witness that night and see if she recognizes him as one of the men dumping something into the dumpster."

"The one on the second-floor apartment?"

Arn nodded.

"She's the first one I wanted to interview when I got this case," Heinz said, "but the old lady had a stroke and died ten years ago."

"Roger," Ana Maria said, leaning closer, "the detective who originally interviewed all of the men noted they were nervous—"

"As I would be," Detective Heinz said, "being married and going to a party where a hooker stripped for money and God knows what else."

"What I'm getting at is that Happ came to the initial interview wearing a heavy coat and gloves."

Heinz nodded. "Detective Barton made a side note of it, and also that the weather was nasty out that day."

C. M. Wendelboe

"Would you have at least taken off your gloves when you entered a warm building?"

Detective Heinz grew silent, looking at Ana Maria like a cow looking at a new gate when he finally said, "Not if I had a serious cut to my hand. You think he was hiding the bandage his wife wrapped his hand with?"

"Perhaps," Arn said, "Happ was hiding a cut from a dumpster."

Heinz picked up the phone, "I'll see if we can overnight samples to Parabon and get a sample to our state lab, though they're overwhelmed with DNA evaluations, too."

"Roger," Ana Maria said softly, "use your best charm for them to expedite it."

6

It had been two days since Ana Maria and Arn had talked with Detective Heinz. This morning, they sat in the kitchen while they talked with the armchair detective, Danny Arron Spotted Horse, who said, "If I were the investigator, I'd plaster Happ St. John's picture all over the TV to see if anyone has any information about his murder."

"That," Arn said, "is why you're not a detective."

Danny flipped sausage links cooking on the stove with tongs and said over his shoulder, "What's that supposed to mean? I think it sounds like a good plan."

"I can take this," Ana Maria said and began educating Danny. "We're certain the killer staged Happ's murder to make it look like suicide. As far as he—or she—knows, the police bought it. The general public thinks Happ killed himself. This way, the killer might become overconfident in his ability to fool the police and eventually slip up. Last thing I want right now is to tip off the murderer about what we've uncovered."

Danny set plates of eggs and sausage in front of Arn and Ana Maria. Arn moved the copy of Josie Dexter's case file aside before diving into his breakfast.

Between the second and third round of coffee refills, the phone rang. Danny grabbed it from the wall and spoke briefly before handing the receiver to Arn. "A Detective Heinz."

Arn took a deep breath before speaking into the receiver. "Tell me you have new information."

"Just from the CBI lab," Heinz said excitedly. "After we talked, I found the blood samples we had from the dumpster still in evidence and blood taken from Happ at the time of his autopsy. It *is* a match. Now, all we gotta do is hear back from Parabon Nanolabs."

"But that's only if we had a suspect to charge," Arn said. "Are you convinced the samples match?"

"I am convinced Happ St. John was one of the men who dumped Josie's body into the dumpster that night," Detective Heinz answered.

"Now, all you gotta do is reinterview all the others at that party still alive and hope one that you interview stands out as the killer among them."

"Unless one of the men who've since passed away was Josie's killer."

"Either way," Arn said, "keep me posted."

Arn hung up and handed the receiver back to Danny. "You didn't shoot texture in that spare room yet have you?"

"My texture gun went south. I was fixing to go to the hardware store and grab another. Why?"

Arn stood with his coffee cup in hand and grabbed Josie's case file. "I have an urge to use a white wall."

Ana Maria and Danny followed Arn down the hallway and

into the small room Danny was currently remodeling. A sheet of dry wall leaned against one wall behind a bucket of drywall mud, and a staple gun hooked to a small air compressor waited for Danny. Arn spread the police reports and interviews on a plywood board laid across two sawhorses and took a Sharpie from his shirt pocket.

"You gonna mess my whole wall up, I bet," Danny said.

"Relax. The texture and paint will cover anything I smear across your precious wall."

Arn began by writing the names of everyone who was there the night Josie stripped at the bachelor party, referring to the original police report, and noting the men who were now dead. He flipped pages and finally said, "There's no mention of who the bachelor party was for."

"Maybe there wasn't a bachelor," Danny said.

"How's that?"

"Perhaps the party was just a pretense to get a known prostitute in a room where the guys could... have some fun."

"He's got a point," Ana Maria said. "It is odd that there's nothing indicating who the bachelor party was supposedly for."

Arn handed Danny the evidence list the tech had filed with the report. "If that's the case—if men paid to have sex with Josie—she should have made a bundle of money from her efforts. I don't see where the evidence tech or the investigator entered any money into evidence. There should have been money in her jean pockets, I would think."

"You figuring robbery as the motive then?" Ana Maria asked.

"I'm not ruling it out." Arn turned to the white wall and began a column with possible motives, the first being robbery.

Ana Maria thumbed through police reports until she came to the autopsy conducted by the Medical Examiner out of Colorado Springs. "Strangulation." She handed the report to Arn. "Much like Happ's death."

Arn studied Josie Dexter's autopsy report. She had been found strangled, her windpipe crushed, her hyoid bone in her throat broken. Bruising along one cheek, the pathologist had noted, appeared to indicate she had put up a struggle before she passed out and was ultimately killed. "Different strangulation," Arn said, "different attack. Happ's killer attacked him from behind but his windpipe wasn't crushed. Had to be a strong person. Also, Josie's killer faced her as he strangled her, the pathologist noted. Though it's not conclusive, I would say there were two different killers."

Danny overturned an empty dry wall bucket and sat next to Arn. "Unless it *is* the same person, and they just perfected their technique through the years."

Arn turned and faced Danny. "That's a pretty profound observation."

"You been binge-watching *Forensic Files* again?" Ana Maria asked.

Danny shrugged. "Does it show?"

Arn said, "Danny might be onto something. I'll call The Ass tomorrow and see just how many strangulation victims Metro has had in the past thirty years."

"This is interesting," Ana Maria said as she held the police report so the light didn't glare on it as she read. "That witness living on the second floor overlooking the alley—Helen Johnston—saw very little of the two who dumped Josie's body. She said the alley light was burned out."

"We knew that," Arn said. "As I recall reviewing the case when I first got to Robbery-Homicide, she didn't get a look at either of their faces."

"But do you recall that she saw that one had a distinct tattoo?"

Arn snapped his fingers. "Forgot about that."

"Holy crapola, Batboy," Danny said. "The omniscient ex-detective Arnold Anderson actually admits he forgot something?"

Arn ignored Danny and turned to Ana Maria. "Forgot my glasses, too. Read it to me."

"Helen Johnston," Ana Maria began, "told Detective Barton that one of the suspects—not the one who cut himself on the dumpster but his partner—had an eagle tattoo high on his right arm."

"Odd," Arn said. "Detective Barton noted on his report it was early October and only thirty-four degrees that night. Let's see that."

Arn took the report from Ana Maria and held it at arm's length just as Danny handed him a pair of pink-rimmed glasses. "Use mine. They're from the Dollar Store but it's better than you squinting like you're Mr. Magoo."

Arn stood and leaned against the wall. He donned Danny's glasses and said, "At a dollar for the pair, I think you got took."

Danny held out his hand. "Then hand them back."

"Soon as I read this." Arn re-read Helen Johnston's witness statement, his initials scrawled on one corner where he had first read the case file thirty years ago. Initials of a dozen other investigators who had gotten the file and failed to solve the case. The witness claimed that the two men's faces were turned away as they stuffed the body—later determined to be Josie Dexter—into the dumpster in the alley outside Helen's apartment building. Both men wore long sleeve shirts against the cold, but the one with the eagle tattoo on his arm had his right sleeve rolled up and something tucked under the cloth. "A smoker."

"Who's a smoker?" Ana Maria asked.

Arn tapped the report with his finger. "The guy with the eagle tat was a smoker. I used to roll my pack of cigarettes up in my shirt sleeve just like that when I had the habit. It was the cool thing to do back in the day. Think John Travolta in *Grease*."

"But why an eagle?" she asked.

"Army or some other service perhaps," Danny said.

Arn turned to Danny. "How many vets had eagle tattoos when you were in the Army?"

"A tat like this?" Danny said, rolling up his shirt sleeve and showing them a years-old faded eagle clutching a branch of a tree as it sat perched looking at everything. At nothing. "I would guess that about every third or fourth Army man back then had such a tat. We were proud to fight for our country. There were many old-schoolers back in the day with a tattoo like this."

"So, we might be looking at a prior serviceman," Ana Maria said. "But that doesn't help us unless we have a suspect and we can dig into their past, see if they served."

Arn grabbed the carafe of coffee and refilled their cups before picking up the stack of police reports and turning pages. "This is that one case that's always haunted me."

"Because you couldn't solve it?" Danny asked.

"That was part of it," Arn answered as he continued riffling through the reports until he found one he wanted to study. "Mostly, it was thinking about that six-year-old girl left an orphan. Her whole world revolved around her mother and suddenly she was left with no one. Here..." He handed the report to Ana Maria.

She brought the police report close to her when Danny handed her his glasses. "Time to admit you're getting old enough to need—"

"Don't you dare say it." Ana Maria took off the reading glasses and read the report. "First the child knew something was wrong was when a uniformed officer and a Family Services worker showed up at her apartment and took her away." She handed the report back to Arn. "Jenessa."

"An unusual name," Arn said, "but one that's stuck with me through the years."

"An unusual name, indeed," Ana Maria stood and headed for the door.

"Little early for you to be headed to the TV station."

Ana Maria stopped and said, "Jenessa. What're the odds—"

"Odds of what?" he asked.

"That the newly appointed Cheyenne Police Detective Jenessa Wells and *Josie's* Jenessa are one and the same? I'm headed to the library. I can access Denver Clerk of Court records from there. Just to satisfy a long-shot curiosity."

7

Ana Maria drove her VW around the circular driveway, the pebble-stone drive's crunching loud inside the tiny car. "Pretty snazzy place for someone who's a seamstress." Arn motioned to a BMW parked in the garage. "No less snazzy than that ride. Must have cost Maddy a mint."

"That's Jenessa's car," Ana Maria said. "She doesn't trust it parked at the police parking lot and leaves it here while she drives her beater Honda to work."

"Still, this place speaks of more than a seamstress."

"Oh, Madeline Wells is much more than just a seamstress." Ana Maria climbed out of the car and stood looking up at the twin columns guarding the entrance to the house. "She is literally the tailor to the stars. She's made suits for De Niro and Clint Eastwood. Now she keeps her business local. Hates traveling, one of her friends told me. Now she just sticks close to Cheyenne."

"That's 'Maddy's Place' down on 16th street across from The Wrangler?" Arn said, finally realizing who Maddy Wells was. Her tailor and dress shop opened long before Arn moved back

44

to Cheyenne ten years ago. Catering to a clientele requiring the finest tailored clothing for their professional life, Arn had always figured he didn't need anything so perfect and had always opted for off-the-rack sport coats at JCPenney. Or Goodwill.

As Ana Maria led Arn up the long sidewalk, the door opened and a stout, middle-aged woman opened the door. Dressed in anything but tailored clothes—with her baggy sweatpants and rolled up sleeves—she looked as if *she* shopped at Goodwill. With her dark hair graying in streaks on the side of her head and wearing no makeup that Arn could see, he instantly liked the woman for her unpretentiousness. *Let the damn world take me as I am*, she seemed to be saying. "My assistant said to expect a reporter from the TV station, but I can't imagine what you would want to talk with me about."

"Happy St. John," Ana Maria answered.

Maddy shrugged. "I heard he was murdered down in Denver last week. But what's that got to do with me?"

Ana Maria explained that Happ's ex-wife was living in Cheyenne, and Ana Maria was doing a follow-up to her broadcast since Happ had a Cheyenne connection, even though he and Sheila hadn't seen one another for thirty years. "Since Happ was a suspect in your sister's murder, I thought I'd get your reaction to his death."

Maddy dropped her head. "How did you know Josie was my sister?"

"Court records," Ana Maria said. "I did some research into Denver records and found you were Josie's only living relative. And that you were gracious enough to adopt her little girl."

When Ana Maria had returned to the house from her research, she had been giddy. "I knew a name like Jenessa was too unusual. *Josie's* Jenessa and the *Cheyenne PD's* Jenessa are the same. Let's go talk with Maddy," she'd told Arn.

"May we visit further inside?" Ana Maria asked.

"We better," she said and looked past Ana Maria. "Who is this with you?"

"Arn Anderson, ma'am—"

"Cut the 'ma'am' bullshit and just tell me who this is hanging around with a reporter."

Arn stiffened and took a deep, calming breath. "I am a retired Denver Metro Homicide detective. I—like all officers new to the division back then—tried to solve the case of Josie Dexter's murder."

"But you never did," she said with a distinct accusatory tone.

"Apparently," Arn answered. "Now, I mainly hang around with my friend Ana Maria and give her police insight. When she'll listen to me."

"I suppose you're harmless enough. Come on in."

Maddy held the door until they'd entered the house. "Follow me and forget the mess in the rooms."

They walked down a long hallway lined with photos of a child developing into a young woman. Arn stopped beside a shadow box with old pistols displayed behind the glass. A large canvas print of a uniformed police officer hung beside the shadow box.

"That's Jenessa the day she graduated from the police academy in Douglas," Maddy said. "I don't have to tell you how proud I was of her that day. Come."

She led Arn and Ana Maria into a room filled with bolts of

cloth and spools of every color thread imaginable as if Maddy's business were run out of her home. "We can talk while I do some work. Have a seat, if you can find one under all that material."

Arn spied a cleared spot on the sofa at the same time as Ana Maria, but she was quicker, leaving Arn to gather several bolts of cloth from an occasional chair and lay them aside before sitting.

Maddy sat in a straight-backed red paisley chair and grabbed a project from the floor. She said nothing as she slowly ran a thick needle through heavy leather when she saw Ana Maria looking at her. "I bet you're wondering what I'm doing sewing at home when I could tell any one of a dozen employees to do this."

"It did cross my mind, actually," Ana Maria said. "For someone to own a tailor shop like you do, with your reputation and the number of seamstresses working for you, you still have to bring work home?"

Maddy laughed easily. "Not that I *have* to but that I *want* to. I was sewing everything by hand when I first started my business, but through the years of modernizing my shop and building my clientele, I didn't have to anymore. But this," she held up the thick material, "keeps the hands supple and strong. I take work home now and again from selected special customers. This one's an elk-hide vest a customer wants when he goes to the Mountain Man Rendezvous at Ft. Bridger next summer."

She set her project aside. "But you said you were doing a follow-up story on Happ St. John's murder and not on the origins of Maddy's Place tailor shop. While you're at it, tell me how you learned about me adopting Josie's little girl, not that I was trying to hide it. It was a private matter—no reason for the public to know, nor that nosy Mrs. Brown who was always coming over to check on Josie and Jenessa."

Ana Maria dug a long, slim reporter's notebook from her handbag and flipped to a clean page. "To answer your question, Jenessa's name is what tipped me off," Ana Maria said. "When I started reading the Denver police report on Josie's murder, there was mention of Family Services taking Josie's girl the morning of the homicide. Jenessa Dexter. I hear that name some mornings when I show up for the press briefing at the police department where a detective Jenessa Wells holds the briefings and that got me curious. So I checked court records and found out that you and your husband adopted her right after Josie's murder. You both must have loved Jenessa tremendously to do that."

Maddy stood and walked to where a photo book leaned against a bookcase and brought it back. She handed it to Ana Maria. "That's Jenessa in there, from even before she came to live with us. We never could have children, Milt and me, though we tried for enough years."

Ana Maria thumbed through the photos, taken from when Jenessa was a baby through her school years. She pointed to a man sitting with Jenessa on his lap, his leather dee strap across his shoulder securing his revolver against anyone grabbing it. "Was your husband a law officer?"

"He was a gate guard with the railroad when we lived in Denver, so we could afford to take Jenessa in after... my sister's murder." Maddy massaged one hand with the other. "It completely devastated Jenessa. My sister was her whole world."

"Must have been hard on her when her momma went out working the streets at night, too."

Maddy picked up the vest and resumed sewing. "That was a bone of contention between Josie and me. I tried to get her to quit the business, but the money was too easy. I told her she didn't know who the hell she would be alone with, but she laughed it off." Maddy's eyes teared up and she looked away. "Guess that last john she serviced was the one I had warned her about."

"Tell me," Arn said while he leaned closer to Maddy, "how closely did you follow the investigation?"

Maddy brushed her hand across her eyes and sat back in her chair. "Closely, at first. I checked in every day for that first several months, though I can tell you there wasn't much of an investigation, if you ask me. Oh, the detective interviewed everyone who was at that last bachelor party, but no one knew a thing. They were all only concerned about would happen if it was leaked to their wives that they were at a party with a known prostitute. Hell, they did more of an investigation when Milt got tanked-up and did that double-gainer off our fourth-floor balcony than with my sister's murder. Guess some streetwalker didn't warrant a lot of attention."

Ana Maria flipped to a page in her notebook and said, "Your husband falling to his death when Jenessa was only nine must have been another blow to the little girl."

"A blow," Maddy said, "and an upheaval. I knew it was only a matter of time before her mother's murder would get around to other school kids and she'd get bullied. Lord knows she got hassled enough in school for that time Milt got arrested for DUI. I had asked Milt to transfer out of Denver for just that reason because the kids were so mean to Jenessa, but he would have

49

none of it. He loved his job and the pay was good. After Milt died, I had no roots in Denver. He had a small life insurance policy with the railroad, enough that I could pack up Jenessa and move here to Cheyenne. Start a business where there was less crime and no income tax."

Ana Maria grabbed her pencil from behind her ear and jotted notes. "How well have you been following your sister's case since it was reopened and sent to the cold case detectives?"

Maddy shrugged. "The Denver news said they had reopened it, but I gave up paying attention to it long ago. I figured they were never going to solve it anyway and I moved on. Why?"

Ana Maria looked at Arn: the time had come for him to be the bearer of news that would bring more bad memories to Maddy and Jenessa. "The cold case detective—Roger Heinz— asked the testing lab for a DNA comparison with Happ St. John and found out his was the blood lifted that night from that dumpster. Happ was the man the witness saw cut himself on the arm as he and another guy lifted Josie into the dumpster."

Maddy stopped her sewing and looked intently at Arn. "Are you saying that Happ St. John might be one of Josie's killers?"

"A positive DNA match," Arn answered. "Even if he wasn't directly involved with her murder, he was involved in covering it up apparently."

A broad smile crossed Maddy's face. "So, after all these years, one of the men that might have killed Josie has been identified and now murdered. I would call that justice—"

The door opened and footsteps approached. Maddy leaned forward and whispered, "That's Jenessa back from her workout. Please, let me tell her about this. She followed the case when she was growing up almost to the point of obsession. But since she became a law officer, she's never brought it up again."

"We will let you tell her then," Arn said just as Jenessa entered the room.

She stopped in the doorway and took in the scene. "Ana Maria Villarreal… is there a story with my aunt you're working on?"

Ana Maria stood and faced Jenessa. Stocky like her aunt. Wearing sweaty workout clothes that hung on her and not a spot of makeup, she could pass for a bag lady if one dismissed the fanny pack around her waist that Arn knew contained a gun and shield. "There is a story here," Ana Maria said, "but we will let your aunt tell it."

"Tell me what?"

"I'll make some tea, child, and then we will discuss it," Maddy said, a look of gratefulness crossing her face. "You folks know the way out, I think."

8

The next day, Arn's Garmin ordered him around a curved street in Arvada until he arrived at Brookdale Assisted Living. The drive down to talk with Neal Barton had been through heavy metro traffic, and he offered to let Ana Maria tag along. "I got some quilting contest in Burns that DeAngelo is sending me to," she said. "Not only am I going to cover it, he volunteered me to be one of the judges. What the hell do I know about quilts except either they're warm or they're not? On the plus side, when I'm done for the day, I'll do some digging into who the other guys Happ St. John made that investment with. Might give us some insight. But believe me, riding through Denver's scary traffic would be preferable to judging a quilting contest."

Yet, driving in Denver's traffic, heavy like Ana Maria feared, gave Arn a chance to think things through and wonder if there even was a human-interest story with Happ St. John's death for Ana Maria. A streetwalker known to the police working a bachelor party found dead in a dumpster, sadly, was of little interest to most people. It was not unusual for sex workers like

Josie Dexter to get in over their heads, to misread a john. A seemingly harmless yet lucrative offer there. Meeting men they didn't know, some with violent pasts. With Josie, the men she met who had killed her were probably the same men who'd disposed of her body. And with the blood from the dumpster and Happ's for comparison, Happ St. John was definitely one of the prime suspects.

This left, perhaps, two men who even cared about Josie's cold case besides Detective Heinz. One, Arn, because leaving a young child motherless when Josie was murdered still haunted him. And the other was a man Arn would soon talk with who might shed some light on the case.

Arn entered the assisted living facility and asked the receptionist if he could speak with Neal Barton.

The receptionist, a lady graying like Arn in her advancing age, looked up from her *Woman's World* and let her glasses drop by the gold chain around her neck. "Neal? You want to speak with Neal Barton?"

"I do."

A wry smile crossed her lips and she chin-pointed to an adjacent room. "He's in the shuffleboard room. You'll spot him easily—he's the only one sitting there and refusing to move any more than he has to."

Arn thanked her and walked into the spacious room where two teams of elderly residents were facing off in an epic game of shuffleboard. Like the receptionist said, only one resident sat in the corner, glaring at the shuffle boarders while occasionally reading a newspaper. He glanced briefly up at Arm before returning to scanning the *Denver Post.*

"Neal Barton?"

The slightly-built man wearing chinos and a blue-striped knitted vest that seemed tailor-made in its quality looked up at Arn. "If I wasn't Neal Barton, you wouldn't be gawking at me. Who the hell are you?"

"Arn Anderson. I started in Robbery-Homicide a couple years after you retired from Metro."

Neal's face softened and he put his newspaper down before motioning to a chair. "Have a seat, big 'un, and tell me what you want from me. Information, I would guess, for what else do I have to give anyone at this point in my boring life?"

Arn set his Stetson on an end table between them and ran his fingers through what was left of his wispy, blond hair. "I figured I'd come and talk directly with the man assigned to the Josie Dexter homicide. The one that took place—"

"I know damn well when it took place! I remember all the homicides I couldn't solve. But don't accuse me of half-assing it like that hooker's sister claimed. What do you want to know about it?"

Arn knew the feeling. As the one case that he couldn't crack, mention of the Josie Dexter murder brought up deep regrets about not being able to spend more time solving it. "Did you hear that Happ St. John had hung himself more'n a week ago?"

Neal guffawed. "That little weasel wouldn't have the *cojónes* to hang himself. Someone did it for him."

"So, you remember him from your interviews?"

Neal turned his chair and looked over his shoulder as he took a vape pipe out and began puffing on it. "Let me know if one of those damn hall monitors comes slinking around."

"I will," Arn said, wondering if Neal could be kicked out of the facility for vaping.

"Now, as far as Happ St. John goes, as it relates to Josie Dexter's murder, I always felt he knew more than he told me. I brought him in for interrogation three times, and each time he seemed more nervous than the time before. But he wouldn't come off his story that the last he saw Josie was when she was at that bachelor party, stripped down to her pasties and G-string, with a bunch of dollar bills sticking out of it."

Arn explained that Detective Heinz, assigned to the reopened cold case, had Happ's blood analyzed with that found on the dumpster the night of Josie's murder. "The state lab verified it and said it was a positive match."

Neal slapped his leg and winced. "I knew—just *knew*—that little bastard was involved. Who killed him?"

"Detective Heinz and Detective Bass are working together—"

"Bass the Ass," Neal said. "Guess he's still got to work to pay alimony for his two ex-wives."

"Three now," Arn said.

Neal shrugged. "No surprise. It was like the fool joined the Wife-of-the-Month Club. He's still on the job, you say?"

Arn nodded. "He was assigned Happ's suicide case, later determined to be a homicide. You mentioned a moment ago you don't believe Happ St. John hung himself. You have suspicions as to who might have killed him? 'Cause you're right—someone strangled him and staged the scene to look like a suicide. Heads up, hall monitor."

Neal hurriedly slipped his vape pipe back inside his vest pocket.

The lady walking the halls stopped and tilted her head slightly upward. She inhaled the air like a coyote sniffs for carrion before resuming roaming the hills. "That one's the worst," Neal said. "She'll put me in time out, and I won't be able to watch shuffleboard for a month."

"Lucky she doesn't kick you out of the facility."

Neal laughed. "At the prices these people charge? I could be caught having sex with one of these old babes and they wouldn't kick me out. Now, back to who might have offed Happ... I thought you worked Robbery-Homicide at one time."

"Until I retired ten years ago."

"If you were a detective, how come you can't figure out who killed ol' Happy?"

"Why, have you got it figured out?" Arn asked.

Neal smiled wide. "I do. It was the other man with Happ that night at the dumpster. With the cold case reopened, I'd be looking for Happ's accomplice."

"And who would that be?"

Neal put up his hands as if in surrender. "How should I know? I'm not a detective anymore."

Arn's head was on a swivel, a ready accomplice to Neal Barton breaking the house rules as the old man puffed on his vape pipe. "Did you ever connect that tattoo to anyone?"

"What tattoo?"

"The one on the upper arm of the second guy disposing of Josie's body. The one the witness described as an eagle perched on a branch."

"Just another tat. I thought military at the time, though I developed no leads from it."

"Did you check with the Army, maybe the Marines, to see if such a tat were common to any particular unit?"

Neal pocketed his pipe and glared at Arn. "Josie Dexter was murdered way back in the day—we were just a little overworked. That was during the period when the mayor and councilmembers all wanted to cut the city budget. We had only so much time we could spend on any one homicide or suspicious death before we were assigned another one. Understand?"

Arn understood. It was the same way when he worked investigations and his captain put constant pressure on him to move on to another case if there was no progress in the first forty-eight hours. But unlike Neal, Arn bulled-up every time the captain pressured him to move on and earned himself a few more days to make more progress. Every victim—whether it be a state senator or a streetwalker like Josie—deserved justice.

And a thorough investigation.

Something Arn was quickly realizing did not happen in Josie Dexter's case.

9

A na Maria pushed her plate away and leaned back from the kitchen table. "You feed me like that again and I won't be able to *buy* a date."

"Darlin'," Danny said, "anytime you get tired of my lasagna and want me to fix you peanut butter and jelly sandwiches, you just let me know."

"Don't tick him off," Arn said while he slid a spatula under another small square of pasta. "I, for one, do not want to eat PB and J sandwiches for supper. Or any time."

"At least one of the three amigos appreciates a gourmet meal," Danny said, gathering up their plates and loading the dishwasher. He turned to Ana Maria and said, "It would probably bloat you beyond attractiveness to a suitor, but would you be interested in a crème brûlée?"

Ana Maria seemed to ponder that for a long moment. "Only if you guarantee you made it from scratch."

"What, you think I bought a Marie Callender's dessert?" Danny held up his fingers in the shape of a cross. "Bite your tongue, kid."

"I'd bite into that brûlée if you'd bring it and a mug of coffee into the spare room." Ana Maria motioned for Arn to follow. "We'll talk shop."

"Don't you guys say one blessed thing about the case until I get in there," Danny said.

Ana Maria and Arn went into the spare room, now almost set up like a command post with the white wall, several colors of Sharpies, and chairs arranged around a sheet of plywood Danny had laid across two sawhorses. He entered the room fighting to keep his grasp on three dessert bowls and a carafe of coffee. He set all at one end of the plywood and sighed deeply. "Thought I'd never make it in here in one piece. What were you guys saying just now?"

"I was telling Ana Maria that Neal Barton had devolved into a crusty old man, but that he was once a very good investigator. Spoon, please."

Danny handed Arn a spoon and slid a bowl of crème brûlée across the plywood to him before he handed Ana Maria her dessert. "If he was so good, why didn't he solve Josie Dexter's murder? Unless he half-assed it 'cause she was *just* a streetwalker."

"Can't really fault him," Arn said. "Investigators get cases that—if they can't develop leads in forty-eight hours—they're forced to pick up the next case assigned to them and run with it. I would bet that you're right, though, that Josie's status was so far down the priority list that Neal Barton didn't even give it forty-eight hours before he tossed it aside and started on a case he felt was more… important."

Danny clutched his bowl and walked to the white wall to study the lists Arn had drawn before. "With Happ dead, that leaves five men still alive who last saw Josie at that bachelor party, any one of whom could have been the other man at the dumpster that night. I'd say the odds of catching Josie's murderer just got better."

"Who says we're trying to catch Josie's murderer?" Arn said. "This started as a simple story about a guy committing suicide with his former wife living in Cheyenne…"

"Who just so happens to be a person of interest in Josie Dexter's murder." Danny turned to Ana Maria. "I hate the term 'person of interest' unless you're talking about a Playboy centerfold. Now *that's* a person of interest. That, and all the wives of those men."

"How do you figure the wives to be suspects in Josie's death?" Ana Maria asked.

"Because," Danny answered, "any wife of any of those men who attended that party should be a suspect. What would *you* do if you were married to a guy who you found out was cozying up to a hooker? Could've brought home an STD? Some women might take serious umbrage at that."

"Danny's right," Arn said. "We have to consider the wives and ex-wives of those men. Maybe we ought to forget the whole thing, as involved as this is getting."

Danny swiped brûlée off his upper lip. "What did all the investigators think when they interviewed the wives back in the day?"

Arn shrugged. "Can't say as anyone ever did. Neal Barton made a side note in one of his reports that he went out of his way to make sure none of the wives found out. He assured the guys he'd brought in for questioning that he didn't intend to talk to their wives. No need at the time, apparently. But you're right, the wives—the ones still living after all these years—might have some insight. I'll call Roger Heinz tomorrow and mention it to him, not that it matters much to me."

"Arn," Ana Maria said, "this was the one case you couldn't crack. The one case that's haunted you, and you claim you have no interest in solving it?"

Arn looked way, but it was too late. Ana Maria knew him too well. He admitted to himself some days ago that—even though he was no longer on the job—he wanted in the worst way to find Josie Dexter's killer. If that meant he would have to help find Happ St. John's murderer to get there, so be it. What else is a retired cop going to do with his time? Not like he could join that quilting class Ana Maria covered or hit the bingo circuit with Danny. Detectives *detected* and Arn figured he was stuck with that obsession for as long as he was on this side of the grass.

He turned back and faced Ana Maria with a drop of brûlée on her chin. "All right, you roped me into another one of your sensational stories. But I have to tell you, any leads to Josie's killer likely died when Happ was murdered. If he would have only named his accomplice before he died—but it appears his murder is a dead end, too."

"Not so fast," Ana Maria said. "You haven't asked what luck I had this afternoon."

"I know what luck you had," Arn said. "You were stuck judging a quilting contest."

"That lasted only half the afternoon, leaving me time to dig into Happ St. John's finances before I had to go back to the station and report to DeAngelo how the contest went."

Ana Maria unzipped a leather file folder and laid out papers on the plywood. She reached into her purse and withdrew a glass case that she opened.

"Took my advice and went to the eye doctor, I see," Danny said.

Ana Maria put the reading glasses on and said, "Walgreens. Eleven bucks. But never mind my glasses… look here." She pointed to a spreadsheet that she had highlighted with a yellow marker. "Happ entered into an investment with three other guys shortly before Josie Dexter's murder."

"How'd you manage to get this specific information?" Arn asked.

"Colorado," Ana Maria answered, "requires that all tontines be registered with the courts."

"A what?"

"A tontine," Danny answered, setting aside his bowl of dessert. "It's an investment scheme whereby each person in the investment group puts up an equal sum of money and leaves it to draw interest. The members receive a quarterly or yearly annuity payment. When one member of the tontine dies, his or her portion of the funds reverts to the surviving members."

Arn stared, amazed at the frail Lakota picking up empty bowls. "How do you know these things?"

Danny shrugged. "I just know things. More coffee?"

Arn shook his head and held out his coffee cup.

"Danny is spot-on with his brief explanation." Ana Maria set that spreadsheet aside and picked up another one with her notes. "I slipped into Mel Gates's office—"

"The TV station's staff attorney? The married man who wants to slip into *you*?"

Ana Maria nodded and smiled wryly at Arn. "I fended him off once again. But I had to see him and have him explain this investment scheme. According to him, it's unbreakable. The only way to get out once you sign up is in death."

"Then that leaves out Sheila and the wives of the other three, it would appear," Arn said. "They would be ineligible for any money upon their husbands' deaths."

Danny said, "I'd be looking over my shoulder if I were the other investors."

"As would I," Arn said. "Does the state require all investors to be registered?"

"Thank goodness they do," Ana Maria said, "or I wouldn't have found out the other three. Look here." She spread three separate sheets out onto the plywood. She explained that Happ and three close friends, Gene Woods, Eddie Bragg, and Haven Talish, all entered into the tontine. "Gene's the one—has that masonry business—that Roger Heinz came up here to interview about Josie's murder."

"And Gene and Eddie were at the bachelor party that night," Arn said recalling the police report. "What about Haven Talish?"

"Looks like he dodged a bullet in the Josie Dexter interrogations," Ana Maria said, picking up a Sharpie and walking to the white wall. "He had an airtight alibi, at least according to one of the investigators who thought there was a connection and interviewed him. It would have been terrible for a gubernatorial candidate to get caught up in that."

Arn had never met Haven Talish, but his name—along with campaign fliers—had been seen everywhere from store checkouts to volunteers going door-to-door, handing them out.

DeAngelo even put up a campaign ad on the television, though Arn didn't pay a lot of attention.

"Might as well scratch him from the suspect list," Danny said.

"Don't do that yet," Arn said. "Not until we prove he was not at that bachelor party. We can prove that, right?"

Ana Maria shuffled reports and came out with a faded one filed by one of the unfortunate new investigators who got the case dumped on them some years after Arn retired. "Like this report says, he was out of town when Josie was murdered, so he wasn't on the list of people interviewed by Neal Barton at the time of Josie's death. Do you remember him from when they dumped the case on you at Metro?"

Haven's name had never come up in Josie's investigation. Still... "Three of the four tontine members—including the now-dead Happy St. John—were at that bachelor party. I can see why Haven wasn't interviewed right off if he could prove his alibi."

Ana Maria dropped that police report onto the thin file representing Josie Dexter's death and shook her head. "The woman deserved more—"

"That's why you, like Arn, are obsessed with finding her killer?" Danny asked.

Sadness overcame Ana Maria's face as she continued looking at the police reports. Though Josie's case had been given to numerous junior investigators upon assignment to Robbery-Homicide, there was little to show that anyone really cared who had killed her. "I stopped by Sheila St. John's house after I finished at the TV station to run Gene Woods and Eddie Bragg and Haven Talish by her. They were the three who hung with Happ—which was understandable. If they were chums enough to trust one another to set up that investment scheme—they were bound to be good friends. Sheila had met them each only once but claimed they all went to every party they could find. Even though it appears the four were inseparable, it looks like Happ, Gene, and Eddie went to that party and ogled Josie Dexter performing her magic for the last time while Haven was out of town. I'll let you dig into and verify that," she said to Arn.

10

Arn entered Maddy's Place, and the aroma of potpourri—a hint of lavender, eucalyptus perhaps—was a soothing accompaniment to Herb Alpert and his Tijuana Brass playing softly from speakers hidden around the inside of the tailor shop. A young girl wearing a Wyoming Cowboy's T-shirt—the black bucking horse on yellow fabric attractive—approached him. Arn asked for Maddy, and the girl said, "She's busy with Mr. Talish but will be finished with the alterations on his suit jacket shortly. Feel free to browse." The girl gave Arn a subtle once-over. "In case you find something you need."

Arn walked around the store until he found the section displaying men's clothing, all tagged *By Maddy*. And all nearly as much as Arn's monthly retirement check. As expensive as the custom designs were, he was surprised Maddy Wells didn't charge a cover price just for looking when she emerged from the back room with a man following her. The receptionist walked to her and whispered under her breath. Maddy looked at Arn walking the aisles, and then said to the man, "I should have the initial fit ready in a week. I'll call."

He thanked her and started for the door when Arn intercepted him. "You're Haven Talish?"

The man stopped. Only slightly younger and taller than Arn, his tanned arms that filled his shirt sleeves showed fitness. "I am Haven Talish," he said, his perfect pearlies showing in his best I-am-running-for-governor smile.

Arn introduced himself and handed Haven a business card. "Why would I need a private detective?"

"You might not," Arn, said, "but one of your old friends could have used one—Happy St. John."

"I haven't seen Happ for many years. Almost forgot about him until I heard he had committed suicide."

"Can I ask you a few questions—"

Haven held up his hand and checked his watch. "I have a meeting with my campaign committee at the Paramount." He handed Arn his own business card. "If you stop by my office when I'm not rushed, we can talk," and he left the shop.

Maddy approached Arn and waved her hand around the tailor shop. "Anything you'd like? I can discount prices twenty percent. Slow time of the year."

Arn laughed. "Even at twenty percent, I'd have to float a loan. Everything I've looked at is impeccable. And out of my price range. Your clients must be very picky."

"*Very.*" Maddy jerked her thumb at Haven leaving the shop. "Like Mr. Talish. He needs a custom suit. Something befitting a gubernatorial candidate on the campaign trail. This morning was his initial measurement session. It's the first time he's been to my shop, and I think he was a little taken aback by my candor."

"Your candor?"

"Yes," Maddy said, "especially when I asked him how it dressed."

"I don't understand," Arn said.

Maddy chuckled. "Apparently, you've never been fitted properly. If you dress left—as most right-handed men do—your tally whacker hangs to the left."

Arn felt himself blush and Maddy laughed even more. "That was the same reaction I got from Mr. Talish, though it truly does effect the way in which I tailor the suit."

"Why would that even be important?"

Maddy paused as if thinking the best way to answer the sensitive question. "It dates back to Victorian times when they factored in how a man... *dressed*. In those times, they went as far as piercing the scrotum and slipping a chain through which was hooked to the man's trousers. Depending on how he *dressed*. Are you sure you don't want a custom suit, Mr. Anderson?"

"I believe I'll stay with off-the-rack sport coats at Kohl's and just figure on dressing somewhere in the middle."

"That was also Mr. Talish's reaction when I explained how involved it is to properly tailor a man a suit, though Lord knows, he can afford whatever I design. I'll have to hustle to complete his order for his fundraising event at Little America next week."

"Fund raising for his gubernatorial run?"

Maddy nodded. "Right before he goes to Jackson Hole to hobnob with the neat and elites, hoping to raise some campaign money."

"His face and name are certainly out there enough."

"He is all but positive he will win this next election and why not?" Maddy said. "He's done the community right with his philanthropy. With as many people in the oil and gas industry as he employs. But you didn't come in here to talk about Mr. Talish."

"Actually, I came here to run a couple names by you—Gene Woods and Eddie Bragg. Know them?"

Maddy nodded. "I know them as being at that last bachelor party my sister worked the night of her death. Apart from that, I do know Gene Woods. He's Cheyenne's foremost mason. He is an artist in brick like I am an artist in cloth. He's done some decorative brick jobs at my house for me through the years. Eddie Bragg, I recall, was interviewed thirty years ago in my sister's murder, but I've never met him."

"Not surprising," Arn said. "He lives the drunk's life in Denver."

Arn stood silent until Maddy asked, "It's obvious you didn't come in here to order a suit or buy something off the rack, so just what else do want from me?"

"Can't lie there," Arn said. He explained that Happ St. John's death triggered in him the renewed desire to find the killer of her sister. "I just have a few questions, if you're up to it."

Maddy shrugged. "Like I told you before, that part of my life is thirty years past. No one will ever find my sister's murderer. I resigned myself to that long ago. But if you feel you have to ask questions I've already answered, fire away."

Arn took out his pocket notebook and flipped pages. "When I was assigned to your sister's cold case when I first got to Metro Robbery-Homicide, there was one side note that another detective had jotted down a few years before I looked at the case file. One thing he was considering was whether your sister was killed by Jenessa's biological father."

Maddy took a step back and crossed her arms like footballers do. "Why would anyone think that?"

"The detective did some digging to find out who Josie's biological father was, though he had no success. He speculated that—if her father were a prominent man, a politician, perhaps—he wouldn't want it known that he'd visited a prostitute. Or, the investigator thought, a married man wouldn't want it known that he had a child out of marriage. Did you have any idea at the time who Jenessa's real father was?"

"First, that's absurd even thinking that. Were that the case, don't you think the man would want that knowledge hidden long before Jenessa was six years old and would have murdered Josie before then to hide it?"

"The detective went further, kicking around the notion that Josie was... blackmailing Jenessa's father—"

"Nonsense. I knew my sister. She'd never do that."

"Desperate people will do desperate things," Arn said, "especially when it means providing for her child." *Especially if you're a hooker having to work the street for whatever money you can bring in*, Arn thought.

Maddy remained silent, glaring at Arn for suggesting Josie had been involved in some blackmail scheme thirty years ago.

Maddy turned away, trembling, her shoulders shaking. "I know nothing about Jenessa's real father, so, please leave."

* * *

"I didn't have any luck finding Jenessa," Ana Maria said. "Apparently when she has a day off, she usually bugs out of town so she doesn't get called in on some case that patrol passes off to her. That's according to one of the uniformed officers. Sounds like I had about as much luck as you did finding out anything useful from Maddy Wells."

Arn thumped his hand against his leg and the waitress looked at him like he was having a Tourette-like outburst. "There's *something* there. The more I talked with Maddy about why it might be important to find Jenessa's biological father, the more upset she became."

"Maybe she became upset because the only father Jenessa really knew was Maddy's husband, Milt. I can see her not wanting to dredge up anything that would spoil Jenessa's memories, even if she only knew Milt a few years before he had his fatal accident."

Arn motioned for the waitress. She refilled their coffee cups and Arn waited until she left before saying, "I have this gut feeling—"

"And it's an ever-expanding gut—"

"…that Maddy knew Jenessa's father. The detective a few years before me thought Josie might be pressuring Jenessa's real dad for support. In his report before passing the case on to someone else who couldn't solve it, he brought up the possibility of Josie blackmailing Jenessa's father."

"I suppose it's not much of a jump from working johns on the street to wanting a better life for you and your child and doing just that," Ana Maria said. "But you'll have a hell of a time finding Jenessa's father. When I researched the Denver records and found where Maddy and Milt adopted Josie, the name of the father was absent on the birth certificate."

"I just know—"

Ana Maria laid her hand on Arn's. "Listen, I know this is an intriguing idea, that Josie Dexter was killed by Jenessa's father after Josie blackmailed him, but we have no proof Josie did anything close to that, do we? For all anyone knows, Josie herself might not have known who the father was. A streetwalker's bound to service dozens of men a week. Maybe that's why the father was never named."

Arn shook his head. "You're probably right. It was mere speculation from the detective working the cold case at the time. Probably nothing more than clutching at straws. Lord knows I had a whole collection of straws when I was assigned it back in the day. Pure frustration at the time."

"Perhaps we ought to leave it at pure speculation," Ana Maria said. "Unless new information surfaces."

Arn agreed. "Unless new information surfaces."

11

Haven Talish's receptionist stood dressed in a demure sand-colored pantsuit, her graying hair pulled back in a tight chignon held together by a turquoise hair tie. She was neither friendly nor hostile and showed no emotion as she handed Arn's business card back to him. She motioned to a waiting area and to a Keurig machine with the coffee pods in a carousel beside the pot. "I will tell Mr. Talish you wish to speak with him."

Arn selected a pod of "Black Rifle" coffee and started the machine as he eyed a plate of Crumbl Cookies calling his name from beside the coffee machine. He resisted the urge to pick one. For all of five seconds when he gave in and selected one. He sat in a plush chair as he nibbled on the cookie and sipped his coffee while he looked at the photos lining the walls. He had researched Haven Talish's history with the Chamber of Commerce and learned that he had invested heavily in oil and gas exploration shortly after he moved here from Denver. His intuitive knowledge of the energy industry landed him numerous oil and gas leases, mainly around Gillette and

Casper. Now, he appeared comfortable sitting back, reaping the benefits, and he hadn't placed a bid or pursued new leases in the last five years. Leaving him time to launch—if civic people were correct—a successful campaign for the governor's mansion.

"Mr. Anderson." Haven Talish stood framed in the doorway, his wide shoulders brushing the sides of the door jamb, standing in a burgundy sport coat with matching tie. "I have a few moments. Please. Step into my office."

Haven led Arn into the office and he was taken aback to see that no photos of Haven's gas and oil conquests hung on the walls. Instead, one wall was lined with Philadelphia 76ers memorabilia, photographs, and newspaper articles dating back to when they were the Syracuse Nationals. Another wall showed Philadelphia Eagles photos and a banner from when they won Super Bowl LII over New England, the final score—41–33—in bold on the front page of the *Philadelphia Enquirer.*

Another wall had been decorated with Phillies memorabilia when they won the 2008 World Series over Tampa Bay.

The fourth wall in the spacious office showed Haven's adoration of the Philadelphia Flyers, one newspaper article bragging the hockey team winning over the Bruins.

Haven walked to stand beside Arn and placed his hands on his hips. "Pretty awesome, huh?"

Arn smiled. "If I didn't know better, I'd say you were a sports fan."

"Guilty. A die-hard Philadelphia fan. It is my one vice."

"Apart from going to parties at strip clubs?"

The smile faded from Haven's face. He motioned to a chair in front of his desk before he slid a coaster close for Arn's coffee cup. His overstuffed chair seemed to swallow him up as he leaned back and said, "This is about Happ St. John's suicide, isn't it?"

"Happ's death was no suicide." Arn explained that Happ was strangled, with the scene staged to look like a suicide.

"News said it was suicide."

"New information emerged," Arn said. "I was hoping you'd have some insight into who might have hated Happ enough to kill him."

Haven tented his fingers as he leaned his elbows on the enormous mahogany desk. "First, let's clear the air—I have not been to a party or to a strip club since I lived in Denver. Those were youthful indulgences, but I grew up quickly when hunger told me I'd better grow up. And I did when I moved to Wyoming—"

"To work the oil rigs in Campbell County around Gillette before moving up to rig foreman and later owning your own workover rig."

"Before I wised up and realized I'd get ahead faster if I took some of that money and invested in wells and equipment. But you have been checking up on me."

Arn grinned. "I had to know where the future governor came from."

"Then you know I invested based on what I was seeing in the oil patch. The other riggers I worked with blew their money on women and the bar scene, but I learned my lesson in Denver and invested smart."

"Buying a workover rig and later a drilling company on a long shot—"

"And scoring big time when the boom took off again in '83."

Haven waved his hand around the office. "Now, my life revolves around politics and going to watch my sports teams. But you came here to talk about the old days when I lived in Denver, not to compare sports teams."

Arn nodded. "Tell me about Happ St. John and those... *old* days in Denver."

"What's to tell? Me and Happ—and Eddie Bragg and Gene Woods—partied. What else do young guys do in their days off but go and have some fun?"

"Have you kept in contact with the others?"

"I see Gene running around town now and again in his company truck is all." Haven leaned over and opened a small fridge. He took out a bottle of Mountain Dew and took a long pull before answering. "Like I said before, the first I'd heard of Happ after all these years was when the news reported his suicide... now a murder, you say?"

Arn slipped his notebook from his back pocket and set his Stetson on the floor. "Killed not a week after Metro Cold Case Division announced they were reopening the investigation into Josie Dexter's murder. That ring a bell?"

"Like Quasimodo," Haven answered. "When I returned from Candlestick Park that weekend, Gene and Happ and Eddie were beside themselves. The stripper they'd hired for a party—Josie Dexter—had been murdered and they had been brought in for questioning."

"Sounds like they were worried."

Haven laughed. "You would be, too, if your wife found out you were there with a prostitute."

"What was your wife's reaction to your buddies being with

a hooker, 'cause I would bet if you guys were close, your wives were close also? Sharing news and emotions."

"I was the smart one," Haven said. "I was the one of our bunch who wasn't married. Still not. I didn't even have a girlfriend at the time. That allowed me to do whatever the hell I wanted, including to go to whatever game I wanted to without a woman nagging me."

Arn flipped pages in his notebook. He had great hopes that Haven Talish would have some insight into Happ's death. And Josie Dexter's murder. "One last thing… you entered into an investment scheme with your three friends when you all were in Denver. With Happ's death, his share reverts to you."

"How did you find that out?"

"Digging into records," Arn said, but left out that it was Ana Maria who had unearthed the tontine scheme. "Point is that, with Happ dead, his portion goes to Gene and Eddie. And you.

"So, what's your point?"

Arn drew in a deep breath, steeling himself. There was just no polite way of saying, "Happ St. John's death is profitable for you."

"And the other two," Haven said again. "None of us had any retirement plan from work back then, so we all agreed to chip in a few lucky bucks in order to have some kind of nest egg when we retired." He stood and checked his watch. "I am afraid I have to shuffle you out… I have the chairman of the party dropping by."

Arn stood and dropped his empty Styrofoam cup in the trash can beside Haven's desk. "If you happen to think of anything at all, anyone who might have had grief with Happ St. John—"

"…I will call you, Mr. Anderson."

"—and anything they might have told you about Josie Dexter at the bachelor party that night."

As Haven ushered Arn out of his office, he stopped beside the wall featuring Philadelphia Eagles memorabilia. He tapped a small photo frame. "That was my ticket to their game against the 49ers."

Arn donned his reading glasses. The date—October 2, 1994—was printed on the ticket. "Must have been a memorable game to enshrine the ticket on your fan wall."

"I hope to shout it was memorable. While Gene and Eddie and Happ were busy watching a stripper at that bachelor party, I was watching the football game. The Eagles barely squeaked by for the win. To say everyone in the stands was on the edge of their seats is an understatement."

"I've been to games just like that," Arn said, heading for the door. "Please call if you think of anything."

12

Arn pulled to the curb behind a flatbed trailer piled high with brick adjacent to the job site. As he climbed out of his car, the wonderful Wyoming wind kicked up, blowing cement dust over him, and he closed his eyes for a moment before grabbing his bandana from his back pocket and wiping the dust from his face. A young guy stripped to the waist, sweaty and looking like someone had dusted him with a sack of flour, walked to the flatbed and to grab a bag of mortar.

"Is Gene Woods around?"

"In the pit," the kid said, not missing a beat as he headed towards where three other men were bent over a pile of brick. "I'll tell him some old dude wants him."

The *old dude* leaned against his car and turned his back to the wind pelting him with dust and gravel when a strong hand clamped on his shoulder. "My mule said there was some guy wanting to talk with me."

Arn turned and looked down at a man who was inches shorter than him but half-again as wide as Arn. He thrust out his callused hand and Arn shook it, the fingers like sausages, his skin rough as a sheet of sandpaper. He motioned to Arn's car and said, "Gene Woods. This your ride?"

"It is," Arn answered. "Can we sit inside out of the wind?"

"Just my thoughts." Gene squeezed himself into the passenger's side of the Oldsmobile, and Arn slid into the driver's seat and turned to face him. Gene snatched a bandana from the breast pocket of his bib overalls and wiped dirt and sweat off his face. "Wondered when you'd be around to talk."

"Did someone tell you?"

"Haven Talish," Gene said. "I ran into him when I was having lunch at the Cosmopolitan."

Before Arn could admire Gene about being at Cheyenne's swankiest restaurant, he said, "I clean up now and again and have a meal at some decent place."

"Never thought otherwise," Arn lied. "What did Mr. Talish tell you I wanted?"

Gene spit dust into his bandana and pocketed it. "He said you were interested in the time we all lived in Denver."

"Lived and partied together, from what I've gathered."

"Lordy, didn't we?" Gene smiled as he relived the good times in his mind. "Seems like every Monday at work I'd have this huge hangover from the weekend before, but we were all young back then. I cannot even imagine partying now every weekend and many weeknights and trying to recover enough to go to work the next day."

"Speaking of work, what made you move to Cheyenne?"

"Don Baker," Gene answered. "He was the master mason I apprenticed with in Denver. I learned the brick trade when I was in the Seabees during a stint in the Navy and wanted more. After

I got discharged, Don said he'd teach me the ropes if I promised not to start a competing business there. I worked for Don, more like an indentured servant as I learned to lay brick. So when Haven called and said people were begging for someone willing to work brick in this part of Wyoming, I moved here and hung my shingle out, so to speak. Been doing good for nearly thirty years. But you really don't care about what brought me here. You want to know about… the party. The one where that girl stripped for us."

Arn remained silent. He had long ago learned that—given the chance without interruptions—most people would open up. Often giving more information than with direct questions. Arn was right.

"The Denver news said Happ committed suicide, but Haven said it's now been ruled a homicide?"

"Apparently."

"Why would anyone kill Happ? Unless, maybe he got into drugs or something shady in Denver?"

"I was hoping you could tell me."

Gene shrugged. "Haven't any idea."

"Then tell me about that bachelor party."

Gene smiled. "That woman Eddie found to strip at the party… Lordy, was she a looker. And that was even before she started taking off her clothes."

"Did you watch her leave the party?"

"Can't recall that I did. Is that important?"

"It is when it was uncovered that Happ was one of two men who might have killed Josie Dexter."

"Whoa! Where did that come from?"

Arn explained that Happ St. John's blood was matched with blood taken from the dumpster where Josie's body was dumped, that he had cut his hand. "Now that you mention it, Happ did follow her out of the house a few minutes after she left. I remember Happ—being a little feller—didn't really catch the stripper's eye, even though he'd dumped half a paycheck into her G-string. Do you think that ties in with his murder?"

"I take nothing for granted," Arn answered. "But Happ may have been formulating a plan to recuperate all the money he'd spent with her. Was it his plan to kill her when he followed her out of the party, or did things just go awry when he demanded... services? We can only speculate." He retrieved a piece of Nicorette gum from his shirt pocket and peeled off the wrapper.

Gene nodded to it. "You quittin'?"

"Already did. Fourteen years ago."

Gene put his head back and laughed. "Lordy, you must still have the urge, just like I did when I used to smoke."

Arn said the desire to light up never left him. "Like a bad habit. Like if I were a partier and that urge to go out and raise hell never left me, was always tugging at me."

"Unless you had a wife holding you back," Gene said.

"What did your wife say when she learned you were partying with a known prostitute?"

"She never found out; I've never told her. Even now, she'd have my *cojónes* in a jar above the mantle. Nowadays, the only partying I do is watching the Super Bowl once a year."

"But you were married back then in Denver... didn't your wife care that you went out with your pards raising hell?"

"That bachelor party," Gene said, choosing his words carefully, "was the final straw for me. I told my wife all we four did every week was go bowling and have a few beers afterwards, until we were brought in for questioning about that stripper's murder. We never found out exactly how she died, but for me it was a wake-up call. I had a heart-to-heart talk with my wife and swore never to go to another party with the guys again. But like I said, to this day, she doesn't know I was at *that* bachelor party."

Arn jotted down what Gene told him, the information too important to trust to memory. "Do you recall if there was any money exchanged between Josie Dexter and Happ... beside mere dollar bills stuffed into her knickers?"

"You mean, did he pay to have a roll in the hay with her?"

Arn nodded. "After all, that was her profession and how she made her living."

Gene sat quiet for a moment before saying, "When the party was winding down, Happ asked me for some spare bills, long after the stripper had put her clothes back on. Before she left the party. Now that you put it that way, I'm thinking that Happ pooled what was left of his money with what I gave him and went off somewhere with her."

"Speaking of pooling money, tell me about that investment scheme you ventured into with Happ and Eddie and Haven."

"How'd you find out about that?"

"Public record," Arn answered.

"Not much to tell," Gene said at last, pulling out his bandana and spitting into it again to wipe dust off his forehead. "We all put in $5,000 in the pot and the investment was to pay us a small stipend every quarter. When it matured, it would pay us the full amount including all the interest accrued."

"Split four ways?"

"Of course."

"But with Happ St. John's death, your share went up considerably," Arn said.

"If you want to put it like that."

"I do," Arn said.

"Then you're right. I'll come into a windfall with Happ dead, not that I need the money. I have all the business I can handle, and I have a healthy 401K now."

"Did you keep track of Happ these past years?"

"What are you implying, that I strangled Happ so that I could profit more from the investment?"

"If you want to put it that way."

"I do" Gene said. "You're forgetting the money won't pay out until maturity date is reached and that's another four years."

"But in the event of the deaths of the other two surviving members, the entire amount goes to the sole survivor."

Gene nodded. "That's how it was set up initially. But remember, there're still three members on this side of the dirt."

"If I were you," Arn said, "I'd keep a good eye looking over my shoulder to make sure you're the last man standing."

13

A na Maria came into the house dolled-up, her makeup perfect, her black hair in a Cleopatra cut, looking like she'd just come off the runway. Or just came from her lunch date with the Cheyenne policeman.

"I didn't figure Two Doors Down would have dessert fit for a model," Danny said as he stood and closed the oven door. "How does a nice, fresh torte sound?"

Ana Maria came into the kitchen and draped her handbag over the back of a chair. She patted her stomach and said, "I just had the biggest burger I've ever had, and you want me to add dessert?" She drew in a deep whiff. "You talked me into it. Where's Arn, by the way?"

"I was out back trying to do some repair on my Olds." Arn walked to the kitchen sink and dribbled dish soap over his greasy hands. "That linkage is giving me fits, but I'm determined to fix it."

Ana Maria sat. "You are about as good a mechanic as Michael Jackson was a construction worker." In Ana Maria's previous life growing up with a mechanic father, she had shown an aptitude for repairing old cars, and she had worked for him until he died and his repair shop was sold. "I'll look at the Olds when we get back."

"Back from where?" Arn asked.

"Denver," Ana Maria said, eyeing the torte Danny slipped from the oven. "And before you ask why I'm dragging you two along, I need some advice on a dinner dress at an exclusive shop there."

"Why not ask Maddy Wells to fabricate something special for you?" Arn explained just how old school Maddy was and the quality of her men's trousers.

"Because I can't afford *her* exclusive clothing," Ana Maria said.

Arn dried his hands with a towel before grabbing plates for the torte. "I'm not sure you realize it, but Danny and I aren't exactly the best judges of women's clothing."

"*Au contraire,* my knuckle-dragging friend," Danny said. "I, for one, happen to know quite a bit about exclusive women's fashion." He turned to Ana Maria. "Are you looking for a Versace or de la Renta one-off? Maybe a Dolce and Gabbana from across the pond—"

Ana Maria held up her hand. "I can't afford any of those, but I would appreciate your opinion. And Arn might actually learn something about ladies' fashion in the process."

Arn handed out forks and sat across from Ana Maria. "This lunch date with your policeman friend must have triggered something special in you if you want to spend mega-bucks on a dinner dress."

"Sgt. Ted Ames fancies himself quite the ladies' man, and I'm going to be just one more conquest he could brag about."

"Then why agree to have lunch with him?

"Information," Ana Maria asked. "He claimed to have important information connected with my story about Happ St. John."

"What kind of information?" Danny asked. He grabbed his own notebook adorned with a silhouette of Sherlock Holmes on the front. With each investigation Arn and Ana Maria were involved in, Danny had become more the amateur detective with each case. The only thing missing with the old Indian was the goofy hat and pipe. "Must be something big to go all the way to Denver with the intent of plunking down a sizable chunk of change for a special dress."

When Ana Maria said nothing as she picked at her torte, Arn said, "Well, let's hear it. What information did Sgt. Ames have that was so momentous?"

"I won't say until we see it for ourselves, but it will severely alter our investigation if it proves to be true." She held up her hand. "But don't ask me more 'cause I don't want to say anything else until I am one hundred percent sure." She seemed to coo as she let a bite of torte slide down her throat. "For now, savor Danny's magic. It ought to tide us over until we get to Denver."

*   *   *

With every passing store, Danny said from the back seat of Ana Maria's VW, "Why don't you try that shop?"

"Will you stop your whining already?" Arn said, though he empathized with Danny. When it came time to drive the hour and a half to Denver, Danny—by virtue of his small size—was relegated to the Bug's back seat. Even as small as Danny was, it was all he could do to squeeze himself into the tight space. Arn wasn't sure there was any more room in the front seat as he tugged his knees away from the dash. If the shift linkage on his Olds hadn't locked up, they would have driven to Denver in comfort.

Arn fidgeted around to where he could better talk to Ana Maria. "Danny might be right… We passed half a dozen high-end women's clothiers. I'm hoping you have one particular shop in mind rather than just driving around watching Danny and me suffer in this cramped little car."

"If you hadn't tried fixing your Oldsmobile yourself," Ana Maria said, "it wouldn't still be sitting in the backyard waiting for me to fix your screw-ups… There! That's what I'm looking for."

Arn turned around just as Ana Maria downshifted and motored into the parking lot of Sammy's Club. "Is that what I think it is? A… gentlemen's club?"

Ana Maria smirked. "It is. The most discriminating club in Denver."

She parked the Volkswagen in the lot beside Lincolns, BMWs, and Cadillacs, and shut the car off. "Coming?"

"In there?" Arn asked.

Ana Maria fished inside her purse for cash. "If my information is right, this will be worth the cover charge to get in."

"Let me the heck outta here," Danny said, an excited edge to his voice. "Been years since I've been to a strip club."

"It has been for me, too," Arn, said. "Not sure I want to go in there—"

"Trust me," Ana Maria said. "If what we find inside is true, you will thank me for springing this on you."

Arn smoothed his jeans once he extricated himself from the tiny car and looked up at the story-high club sign. "Hope we're dressed appropriately—"

"I'm more interested in how many dollar bills I have," Danny said, fishing into his jeans pocket while he headed for the entrance.

Ana Maria took Arn's arm in hers and steered him towards the door where Danny already stood waiting for them, clutching greenbacks. "Just try to relax and enjoy the... entertainment. I hear it is world class and not like those sleazy shows you see elsewhere."

"I don't believe you hornswoggled Danny and me here."

Ana Marie winked. "Let us just say it's 'Be Kind to Seniors Day'."

At the door, they encountered a man nearly twice as heavy as Arn, and he wondered just where the hell the guy got his red blazer, tight enough that the pistol under his arm imprinted on the cloth. The doorman looked like he was capable—and prepared—to use the weapon, if necessary. "Three," the man proclaimed without a hint of emotion as he looked at Ana Maria handing over sixty dollars for their cover charge.

Danny looked up at the man and asked, "What do we get for our twenty bucks?"

"A great view of the ladies," the man answered. "And one free drink."

"I don't drink."

"Then tell the waitress you want coffee. Move inside, please."

They stepped inside and Arn moved to one side of the door to allow his eyes to become accustomed to the dim light.

Patrons sat at tables a foot below the stage. One table hosted suited-businessmen casually glancing at a dancer in her G-string, undulating to the soft music, while a man and woman giggled from another table, glancing up at the dancer now and again as if she were the object of some private joke. Arn headed for an empty table in the corner when Ana Maria grabbed him by the arms. "You're not getting off that easy. There's room in front of the stage."

"In the front where the ladies... squat, trying to coax money from you?"

Ana Maria nudged Arn. "Pay when the waitress takes our drink order. And don't cheap out and think you're going to stuff dollar bills into the dancer's knickers. Stuff Lincolns in, at least."

Ana Maria sat between Arn and Danny. She ordered a margarita and Arn a rum and Coke. Danny—being a long-time sober member of A.A.—ordered coffee like the doorman suggested.

The dancer—a girl appearing to be college age—knelt in front of Danny. He grinned wide as he slipped a dollar bill into her G-string. She lingered in front of him, expecting more. When he didn't add to that one dollar, she glared at Danny like he was the cheapest human being on the planet. She sashayed off the stage while Danny looked after her.

The dancing music stopped, replaced with soft elevator music to tide the customers over until the next performance. "That was certainly worth the trip," Arn said. "Ready to head back?"

"We're not leaving quite yet," Ana Maria said.

"I got to tell you," Arn said, "at my age, that girl didn't do a lot for me except remind me how cramped it was riding in your Bug all the way from Cheyenne."

"Speak for yourself."

Arn looked at Danny, his bony elbows resting on the stage. *Is that a spot of drool on his lip?* Arn wondered. "At your age, I'm surprised you didn't have a heart attack." Arn stood and said, "I know an excellent Bohemian restaurant a few minutes away—"

Ana Maria grabbed him by the arm and sat him back down. "Not so fast."

"What are we waiting for?"

Ana Maria checked her watch. "The reason for our little outing. Flambé. She ought to start her performance in about a minute."

"What's a Flambé?" Arn asked.

"You'll see," Ana Maria answered.

Within minutes, disco music started up. Men—and women—seated at tables got up and moved closer to the stage. The doorman eased himself away from the entrance and his attention turned to the pole in the middle of the stage. She emerged from a green and purple fog drifting upwards from vents in the floor. Her hair cascaded over taut breasts, two pasties covering her nipples.

A man moved to sit at the edge of the stage, several fifty-dollar bills ready to stuff into the dancer's G-string.

She turned around and bent over, grabbing her ankles and, when she started working her way up the pole, turned to face the patrons. Her bright red eyes locked on Arn, then Ana Maria, and her undulations and gyrations suddenly seemed *off*, as if she had lost her concentration. She began backing away when cat calls coaxed her closer to the edge of the stage where patrons—including Danny—waited to stuff money into her G-string, and Arn saw for certain... "Tell me that's not Jenessa Wells," he whispered.

"I'd be lying if I denied it," Ana Maria said. "You can hardly recognize her all made-up, huh?"

"My God, she's—"

"Stunning?" Ana Maria said.

"To say the very least."

Danny turned to Arn and said, "Quick, give me some bills," but Jenessa had already begun wrapping up her brief performance. The last thing she did before disappearing behind the curtain was look at Ana Maria and chin point toward a corner table.

The other patrons grumbled at the abbreviated performance that "Flambé" had just given and moved away from the stage back to their tables.

"Let's go wait at that corner table for her," Ana Maria said. "I suspect she wants to talk with us."

After they sat and ordered more drinks, Ana Maria grinned at Arn. "You look like you've just been hit with a sledgehammer."

"More like hit with a pair of panties," Danny said. "You knew Jenessa was an exotic dancer?"

"Not until I had lunch with Ted Ames," Ana Maria answered. "He found out Jenessa danced here on her days off and thought that information would leverage some air-time for one of his cases if he told me. Seems like Sgt. Ames has ambitions of chiefdom when the current police chief hangs up his belt. Here she comes."

Jenessa walked through the patrons who only gave her passing looks with her baggy sweat pants and a torn T-shirt that was big enough to fit Arn. She wore no makeup, and her hair was pulled back in that bun Arn saw the first day he met her. Gone were the red contact lenses she'd just worn for her performance, her eyes once again green. She sat at the table and clutched her diet soda as if it would give her strength to confront them. "Looks like the gig's up. How did you know...? No, don't tell me—that weasel Sgt. Ames. He happened onto one of my performances here last month, but he promised he wouldn't tell anyone."

"Guess he lied," Ana Maria said.

"Damn him." Jenessa looked away. "He came on to me back in Cheyenne a couple of times after he saw me working at the club here. Tried his best to get a date with me and... more, I suspect. There's always more. He even knows about my birth mother being a prostitute."

"From what I've learned," Arn said, "your biological mother did what she had to do to provide for her daughter."

Jenessa guffawed. "And, what, pass on the urge to... entertain men?"

"I don't think what you're doing is because of any hereditary trait."

"Why *do* you strip?" Danny asked.

Jenessa glared at the little Indian. "And who the hell is this?"

"Daniel Aaron Spotted Hawk," Danny answered proudly. "And after that performance, your biggest fan."

"It's safe to talk around Danny," Ana Maria said.

"I don't think it's safe to talk about this around anyone," she waved her hand at the stage. "But now that you know, what are you going to do with the information that Cheyenne PD's only female detective leads a double life dancing in a gentlemen's club? Maybe pressure me into giving you the inside scoop on some case that's newsworthy some time? Is that what you're after?"

"We're not going to do anything," Arn said. "I think I can speak for Ana Maria, but what you do in your off time is your own business."

"Arn's right," Ana Maria said. "But to satisfy my curiosity, just why do you do this?"

Jenessa pointed to the door. "Did you notice all those high-end cars parked in the lot?"

Ana Maria nodded.

"One of those BMWs is mine. Cost me a tad north of two-hundred grand. You think I can afford that on a law officer's salary? It is my one vice—expensive and very fast cars. I have to feed my addiction some way and thought, what the hell, if my mother could strip, I can, too."

She held up her soda can and a scantily-clad waitress brought her another. "Now it's your turn, as even us strippers have their own curiosity—why did you three drive all the way down to Denver, when you could have just come around and asked me if I worked here?"

"If I would have come out and asked you cold," Ana Maria said, "would have admitted it?"

Jenessa thought for a moment before saying, "Without you showing me some proof?"

Ana Maria nodded.

"Not on your life," Jenessa said. "If the chief finds out I dance here on my days off, I'll be out of a job. And though policing doesn't pay a bunch, it does have retirement and medical. Someday, I won't have to do this, unlike my mother the streetwalker, whose only retirement was being murdered and tossed in some filthy dumpster."

Arn finished his drink, feeling lightheaded. It had been ages since he'd had a rum and Coke, and he'd just had two. "If I'm reading you right, your mother's murder is never far from your thoughts."

"Could *you* put it in the back of your mind if it were your mother strangled to death?" Jenessa asked. "Her body found half-naked in a dumpster like some discarded piece of trash?"

"I could not," Arn said. "I'm afraid it would consume me until I found her killer."

Jenessa leaned back in her chair. "And there you have hit it on the head. One day, long after Uncle Milt fell off that balcony— Maddy sat me down and told me about Josie. Uncle Milt wanted to shield me from the truth, always sitting me on his lap and telling me whatever I heard from school kids was a lie about my mother. But Maddy did the right thing in telling me."

"And you've been obsessed with her death ever since?" Ana Maria said.

Jenessa nodded. "Obsessed enough to go into law enforcement. I thought at one time if I could become an officer that might teach me to think like the killer thought that night. It would give me access to police databases. Anything that would lead me to her murderer. But to be honest, after all these years, I have put Josie's death aside. I have finally moved on. Now all I do is investigate property crimes and dance here." She finished her soda and stood. "Once again, what are you going to do with the information that I am Flambé, the premier attraction at Sammy's Club?"

Arn looked to Ana Maria and something knowing passed between them. And with Danny. "Why," Arn said, "we'll just come in and enjoy the show now and again."

"And marvel at the transformation," Danny added, that spot of drool still on the old man's lip.

14

Ana Maria came into the kitchen where Arn struggled to resist a stack of Danny's special blueberry pancakes. Arn lost the fight and handed the old Indian his plate. "You must have smelled Danny's cooking to have lured you from the TV room."

"I wish it was that." Ana Maria plopped down on a kitchen chair. "Denver news just reported another homicide—Eddie Bragg this time."

Arn stopped mid-mouth, syrup dripping off his pancake. "Eddie who was one of those interviewed in Josie Dexter's murder? Who partied with Happ and Gene and Haven Talish?"

"The same." Ana Maria slid her coffee cup closer to Danny, and he filled it. "They're certain it was murder."

"How?"

"Strangulation," she answered. "Seems like everyone from that bachelor party is winding up dead lately."

"Or everyone involved in that investment scheme," Danny said.

After they ate, Arn headed to the TV room. He turned the

television on, but the Denver station spoke no more about Eddie Bragg, as if his fifteen seconds of fame had been snuffed out as quickly as his life.

He punched in Sal Bass's direct number and was unpleasantly rewarded with, "Who the hell's calling my private number?"

"Arn Anderson—"

"How'd you get my number?"

"Important thing is, what's the skinny on Eddie Bragg? How'd he die? Do you have any suspects—"

"Whoa!" Sal said. "You know I can't give out anything on an active investigation."

"Can you at least tell me the headline version?"

Sal laughed. "That I can do. Eddie Bragg—resident drunk of Colfax Avenue—was found with his pockets butterflied, his windpipe crushed, and testing at a .31 blood alcohol level. That's the story. I'm thinking it's a simple robbery gone south. Way I see it, the victim passed out and then the scrote came upon him. The vic woke up while the perpetrator was rifling through his pockets for cash and resisted, whereupon one Eddie Bragg was strangled. Now, that is all I'm going to say," and Sal disconnected.

Ana Maria came into the room and leaned against the door jamb. "What did Bass the Ass tell you?"

"Not much, except he confirmed what the news put out." Arn told her about Eddie's level of intoxication and how it appeared his killer had rifled through the victim's pockets. "Sal was convinced it was a simple robbery gone bad."

"But you're not?"

Arn shook his head, still digesting what Sal had told him. "You know I don't believe in coincidences. I don't think it just so happens that two men—both suspects in Josie's murder—are suddenly found dead a week apart."

"Detective Bass could have shared more information than that," And Maria said. "Like there's bad blood between you two."

"You could say that."

Ana Maria sat silent. She would sit there until Arn explained that… "When I was with Robbery-Homicide, I was sent around Metro to assist other detectives who had run into a brick wall. Essentially, taking their cases over."

"Like a troubleshooter?" Danny asked.

"Sort of," Arn said. "Most of the investigators resented an outsider taking over their investigations, but they relented with little more than a whine. Sal… he went to the police chief and complained, which promptly brought him an ass-chewing and orders to bend over backwards to help me in whatever case of his I was sent in on. All the chief was concerned about was with success in clearing cases, which meant the mayor and city council were off of the chief's butt. Sal still resents me."

"This is his way of enacting little revenge," Ana Maria said before grinning. "Perhaps Roger Heinz will help us. *If* we can convince him it ties in with Josie Dexter's cold case. Punch up his number."

Arn punched up Detective Heinz and put it on speaker phone. When he came online, Arn told Heinz that Ana Maria was with him on the call. After explaining he was looking for more information about Eddie Bragg's death, Detective Heinz said, "That is a current case. Not a cold case, so I'm not privy to much."

"I think it might tie in with Josie Dexter's murder."

"I don't see how," Heinz answered.

Ana Maria lowered her voice in that tone Arn recognized she often used when eliciting information from reluctant people for one of her broadcasts. "Does it not seem odd to you, Roger, that Eddie Bragg and Happ St. John were murdered just a week apart? Right after Metro opened up Josie's cold case. I would bet—as thorough as you are—that you looked Eddie up and interviewed him?"

"I did, but it wasn't much of an interview. I managed to find Eddie staggering out of the liquor store a few days ago," Detective Heinz said, "but he was too drunk for me to ask him about that night of the bachelor party. He was just so schnockered-up, I didn't figure he'd even remember his name. I planned to go back and catch him when he was reasonably sober, but once again, I was too late. Just like I should have brought Happ St. John in before he was murdered."

"Don't beat yourself up over it," Arn said. "An investigator can hardly solve all their cases."

"You did," Heinz said.

"Maybe all the *fresh* cases. But like all the others, I couldn't crack Josie Dexter's," Arn said, then added, "what did you hear about Eddie Bragg's murder?"

Heinz chuckled. "I doubt Detective Bass spent much time on the case, Eddie being a drunk and a druggie. And as emaciated as Eddie looked that day I found him staggering down East Colfax, it wouldn't have taken a strong man to kill him. Especially if he were passed out."

"Detective Heinz... Roger," Ana Maria said, "what would it hurt to get with Detective Bass and find out if there's something there that ties in with Josie's case?"

After a long pause, Detective Heinz said, "All right. I'll brave it and go see The Ass, but only because I'm finding nothing in the cold case files that helps me find Josie's killer. If there's anything connecting Eddie Bragg to Josie's case, I just might call you back."

"Think he'll call back?" Arn asked after they'd disconnected.

Ana Maria smiled. "Of course, he will. Any cop solving a decades-old homicide will be catapulted to national prominence if he's successful. Heinz'll call back. In the meantime, I hope you're occupying your time with something besides screwing up your car any more."

"I think I figured it out. But before I get back to fixing that linkage, I thought I'd go pay Maddy a visit again and see what she knows about Eddie Bragg. How about you?"

"DeAngelo told me to wear some jeans and grubbies to go cover a traditional branding at the Bar Y, north of town. He told my cameraman to make sure he gets some shots of me getting 'down and dirty'."

"Ever been to a branding?"

She shook her head. "What's it like?"

"Work," Arn said. "Hard work. So, be prepared to chip a nail or two."

"Like mechanic-ing on the side doesn't mess up my nails? I'll have Danny pack me a sack lunch."

Arn chuckled. "No need for that. Folks hereabouts usually offer good feed at brandings. You'll get the freshest beef you've ever had. It will broaden your appreciation of Western food. All I can say is *bon appétit*."

* * *

Arn stopped at Maddy's Place, but the receptionist he had talked with earlier was guarded, not wanting to say where her boss was until Arn lied and said, "I wanted to schedule a fitting. I need a new suit for a wedding this summer."

A broad smile crossed the young girl's face. "She called in that she had a terrible headache but will come back tomorrow. Then you can tell her *how you hang*," she winked.

Arn blushed and quickly left the tailor shop, debating if he should drop by Maddy's house. His last conversation with her had not gone well, but he decided to chance it. If Maddy kicked him out of her house just for stopping and asking simple questions, he was prepared for that, too.

He pulled into her driveway and parked. Taking a deep breath, he climbed out of his car and walked slowly to the front door. It opened even before he got to it. Maddy stepped out of the house and closed the door. She guarded the door with her arms crossed and said, "Saw you walking up on the security monitor. What is it now?"

Arn explained that the Denver television station had a brief story on Eddie Bragg being strangled to death.

"What's that got to do with me?"

"I gathered from the few times we spoke that you had kept up on your sister's murder."

"I did at the time back when it happened. Not so much now, as it'll never be solved. Your point?"

"Eddie Bragg was one of the attendees at that bachelor party," Arn said, gauging Maddy's reaction, "and now he was found dead."

"And you think I drove down to Denver, killed Eddie because he was one of those interviewed in Josie's murder thirty years ago, and drove back here?"

"That never crossed my mind," Arn said, but there was something in what she said that lingered in Arn's mind. Something that he would have to think about when he was alone. When he had some quiet time. "I was hoping you had some insight into his death."

"That's assuming I even knew him. Assuming I've kept interested in Josie's murder all these years."

Arn nodded.

"Then, this will be a short visit… I knew Eddie Bragg as one of the attendees at that bachelor party from the original police report thirty years ago. I never spoke with him. Never thought he was any more a suspect in Josie's death than the others who ogled her as she stripped. I always thought she got crosswise with some john, or one of her customers got a little too rough with her, and that's who killed my sister. Now, when the others turn up dead, you can come ask me about them and I'll tell you the same thing."

Arn said he thought nothing bad of her and turned to walk away when Maddy said, "By the way, just what are you going to do with that information?"

"What information?"

"About Jenessa… *Flambé*? About her dancing in Denver?"

Arn faced Maddy. "I hadn't planned on doing anything with it. I take it she told you we saw her at Sammy's Club?" He glanced at the open garage door, but Jenessa's car wasn't there.

"She told me you and that television reporter ambushed her at the club. She was more than a little upset."

"If she's home, perhaps I ought to reassure her that no one in the police department will know she strips beside that Sgt. Ames."

"She had to stay overnight in Denver," Maddy said. "After she saw you and your reporter friend at the club, she was very worried the chief would find out through Ana Maria's broadcast. She started drinking, which she rarely does, and didn't feel like she should drive, so she grabbed a motel for the night."

"Then, when she does get back to Cheyenne, tell her Ana Maria and I intend to tell no one. If she wishes to lead a double life, that is her business."

15

On the way back home, Arn made a detour and stopped by the police department. Officer Smith sat behind the receptionist desk beside the man who performed VIN checks on vehicles. Greg Smith had been one of Arn's first contacts when he'd moved back to town, and the officer frequently... bent the rules when Arn had questions normally restricted to the public. "What is it this time, you want a free gun lock? Maybe one of the publicity brochures we pass out?"

Arn grinned. "Those were my second and third requests."

"What's the first?" Smith asked.

"Sgt. Ames," Arn said. "Is he in the building?"

"He's out on the street, but I can call him in, if it's important."

"Please," Arn asked and sat in one of the overstuffed chairs in the lobby waiting area.

After a few moments of reading *Modern Paternity*, the only magazine on the waiting room table, a uniformed patrolman pulled up in front of the police department and entered the lobby. Arn had never met Ted Ames before, but he'd met the swagger, the self-promoting air, as the sergeant talked a moment with Officer Smith before walking over to Arn. "Whatcha need, old timer?"

Arn forced a grin and motioned to one of the chairs beside him. "I'd like a moment of your time."

"What, you get your car broken into or something? Maybe someone stole something out of it? Lot of that going on, if you don't lock your car—"

"I'm a retired cop," Arn said. "Believe me, I know enough to lock it." He handed Sgt. Ames his business card.

Ames chuckled. "I hope the hell when I retire, I don't have to do PI work. No offense, but I'd rather work at the pepper factory picking fly shit out of pepper when I retire. Maybe work at the sale barn leading blind pigs out to take a crap. PI work? Never, old timer. For me, it's sitting on a beach some place, eyeing the babes."

"That's if you actually live to retirement age."

"How's that?" Ames asked.

Arn motioned to the chair. "Sit, please, and we can talk about one of your detectives, you and me."

Ames sat slowly, cautiously, and leaned closer to Arn. "Which detective?"

"The only one you think about constantly, I am sure," Arn began. "Jenessa Wells. Seems like we share a secret."

"What secret?"

"Come now, Teddy... Can I call you Teddy—"

"Sgt. Ames—"

"...Teddy, we both know that Detective Wells is an exotic dancer in a Denver club on her days off."

Ames smiled. "Is she ever! I heard she does private parties, too. So, you've seen her as well?"

"I have and, like I said, we share a *secret*. *Her* secret. I would like to see it kept *her* secret. She doesn't need any grief from the administration."

Ames shrugged. "She should have been more careful with what she does on her days off."

Arn leaned closer and his voice hardened. "Are you familiar with the Hell's Angels theory of secrets?"

"Can't say that I am."

"They say three can keep a secret if two are dead." Arn leaned closer and met Ames's stare. "In this case, two can keep a secret—that's you and me—and no one need die. Teddy, never tell anyone what Jenessa does on her time off."

Sgt. Ames scooted his chair back and looked around but there was no one else in the lobby waiting room to hear. "I ought to arrest you right here, threatening an officer—"

"And let *your* little secret get out?"

"What secret?"

"That not only do you frequent a gentlemen's establishment like Sammy's Club, but you climb up on the stage with bills between your teeth. Drunk. Trying to put the bills into the dancers' G-strings before the bouncer had to kick you out. Last I knew, police agencies had policies against officers frequenting such places."

"I get it now," Ames said. "You just want to sidle up next to Jenessa yourself."

"For one," Arn said, "Jenessa is young enough to be my daughter, if I had one. Another thing, I do not want grief upon her because some loud-mouthed drunk saw her one night at a strip club and tried to squeeze her for a date. And *then* some.

107

So, if you want to start arresting, skin your cuffs out. If not, take this as a not-so-friendly visit. Keep quiet about her."

*   *   *

Ana Maria shook her head when Danny handed her a custard topped with almond whipped cream. Her favorite. "I don't think I can ever eat again after today."

"I take it you didn't have fun at the branding?" Arn said, dipping a spoon into his dessert as he kicked back in his recliner. "Was it at least interesting?"

"That's one way to put it," Ana Maria said.

"What job did they give you?" Danny asked. "'Cause every branding I was ever at in my younger days, everybody had a specific job to do."

"The ranch hand that was hitting on me said he gave me an easy job since this was my first branding. And it'll be my last."

"What job?" Danny repeated.

"I had to hold the calves' legs while the ranch hand... sliced the nut sack. Do you know how gross it is to see a testicle—or pair of them—pop out and roll on the ground? The poor critter bawling like he was seeing the end of his days?"

Arn knew. As a boy growing up in Cheyenne, he had been farmed out by his dad to local ranchers, who organized their brandings as annual celebrations. Arn could envision a rancher taking his pocketknife and slicing the skin, popping the nuts out, and gathering them up. Handing them to a cook to clean and fry right there over the same fire used to heat the branding irons. "Still doesn't explain why you're not eating

Danny's custard. You know it's world class."

"Thank you," Danny said with a bow before turning to Ana Maria. "Why are you refusing dessert?"

"For the same reason I couldn't eat supper," she answered. "Because I still have that... *taste* in my mouth."

"What taste?"

Ana Maria stood from her recliner as if bugs were in her chair and she shuddered. "The nuts. The testicles! Have you ever had... fresh nuts hot off the calf? Do you know how *gross* that is? The ranch women had a huge fry pan going over a fire and they... cooked up the nuts! Right there in front of the poor calves who just lost them! The ranch hands actually stood in line to get theirs. The cowboys guilt-tripped me into eating one. My cameraman said it would make great evening optics. Do you know how *gross* that is?"

Danny's hand instinctively went to his groin. "It always has seemed pretty barbaric."

"I don't know," Arn said. "Every branding I've ever been to, the women breaded and pan-fried the nuts to perfection."

"Perfection," Ana Maria said, "is leaving the testicles on the poor creatures. But let's talk about something else—my stomach is starting to churn. Did you accomplish anything today?"

Arn explained how he paid Sgt. Ames a visit and told him not to spread around what he knew about Jenessa's dancing on her day's off.

"Did you manage to find Maddy? When you called from her tailor shop, you said she'd called in sick."

Arn stood and motioned for Ana Maria and Danny to follow him. "Let us retire to the spare room. Sure you don't want dessert?"

Ana Maria hesitated before saying, "Well, OK. But make it a big dish, as I need to get this taste of *nuts* out of my mouth."

"Me and my own nuts will be in the room in a wink," Danny said.

He peeled off for the kitchen while Ana Maria and Arn walked into the spare room. The white wall, with the columns of clues and suspects marked with a Sharpie, seemed to mock Arn for not solving the recent cases. That the wall had changed but little these past few days seemed to taunt Arn for his inability to find Josie Dexter's killer thirty years ago.

Arn waited until Danny returned with Ana Maria's custard before saying anything. He had learned long ago the old man's mind was as analytical as any career criminal investigator. More so now that he had been binge-watching *Forensic Files*. He handed Ana Maria her bowl and stood studying the white wall. "I see you've elevated Gene Woods and Haven Talish to top suspects. That's because Eddie Bragg was found murdered, I take it?"

Arn nodded. He had sat in front of the white wall pouring over police reports, and moving Gene and Haven gave him some satisfaction. "That tontine investment scheme. With Eddie Bragg dead, Gene and Haven stand to inherit a sizable windfall when the tontine matures."

"They'll be wealthy," Ana Maria said between spoonfuls of custard. "If they can stay alive long enough to collect it."

"There's another reason to elevate Gene to the top of the suspect list," Danny said. He picked up a Sharpie from the plywood lying across the sawhorses and waved it around like a scimitar. "Gene was at that bachelor party. When Detective Heinz brought Happ in for questioning, he was just nervous enough to be on the cusp of breaking under interrogation. As Gene was nervous when Heinz drove up here to interview him. Maybe Gene was the other man who stuffed Josie Dexter in that dumpster."

Arn looked at the column of suspects and clues. "Or perhaps Gene was nervous because he didn't want his wife finding out. When I talked with him at that job site, Gene said she ruled the roost even now. But you got a point—Gene could be that other man at the dumpster. He was at the bachelor party—the last place Josie was seen alive. He could have heard on the Denver news last week—like we initially did—that Metro was reopening Josie's cold case and got nervous." Arn tapped Gene's name. "With Happ being a little guy, it'd be hard for him to haul a dead Josie very far, back in the day. A strong helper would be needed, and Gene is definitely stout."

"And he could have figured the cold case unit would eventually find Eddie Bragg," Danny said. "Sober, Eddie might have spilled his guts."

Danny placed a star beside Gene Woods' name, their indication that he was higher on their suspect list.

"But he's not the only one who has become a suspect since we last looked at the white wall." Ana Maria licked her spoon, dragging out her explanation like a trained actor when she said flatly, "Jenessa Wells."

"Jenessa?" Danny said. "But she's a law officer—"

"And one who was, at one time, so obsessed with finding her mother's killer that she became a cop," said Ana Maria. "Just because she denies being obsessed with it now doesn't mean she isn't."

Arn set his bowl down and said, "that's a stretch. Jenessa's given no indication she wants to mete out justice herself."

"Is it a stretch?" Ana Maria took the Sharpie from Arn. "Happ and Eddie were both strangled. For someone who works out every day, strangling either man would not be difficult for Jenessa, not like they were big men in life. Especially Eddie, being perpetually drunk. She might have a hell of a time strangling you, but she'd have no trouble with someone... Danny's size, which it appears Eddie and Happ both were."

Danny's hand went to his throat. "I'll put the bowls in the kitchen sink."

Arn shook his head as he studied the wall. "I think you are way off base."

"Am I?" Ana Maria asked. "Where was Jenessa last night?"

"Maddy said she drank too much and didn't want to drive. Stayed over in Denver."

"And when was Eddie Bragg found murdered?"

"This morning according to Denver news. But that's a coincidence, pure and simple."

"Would it be coincidental if she were in Denver the night that Happ was murdered?" Ana Maria turned to her purse and pulled out a slip of paper. "As I was at the branding waiting in line for my prized calf testicle, I punched up Sammy's Club to find out past entertainment. 'Flambé' comes up several times as the headliner. One of those nights a couple weeks ago that she danced was the night Happ St. John was murdered."

Arn's eyebrows raised. "Now that's more than coincidence. Being in the Denver area one night a victim was found murdered is a coincidence. Twice... now that's something to consider.

Mark her down."

"I see the plot thickened while I was in the kitchen," Danny said as he walked into the room. Arn explained how Ana Maria had researched Sammy's Club's past headliners and learned Jenessa in the form of the red-eyed Flambé had been in Denver the nights of both Happ and Eddie's murders. "I hope she's not the killer. I have about fifteen dollars invested in her future from when we saw her perform. But aren't you forgetting someone?"

Arn and Ana Maria looked at Danny like he was talking Swahili. "I think we've included everyone," Arn said.

"Elementary," Danny said, exaggerating an anemic Doctor Watson. "Remember you were just commenting at supper about what Maddy Wells told you when you talked with her today… about you intimating she may be the killer in Denver?"

"I did," Arn answered, recalling that Maddy came up with that facetious accusation on her own. Where had that statement come from unless she actually *were* a suspect, he wondered. "I never really considered her a suspect…"

Arn grabbed the Sharpie from Ana Maria as if he were about to have an epiphany. "But it's such a slight chance…"

"Is it?" Danny said. "Josie Dexter was Maddy's sister and she kept abreast of the case after it happened, bugging Neal Barton every day to prod the investigation along. It's not a stretch with her, either. She was shopping in Denver when Happ St. John was killed, right?"

"For fabric," Ana Maria said. "I can show you the exact shop." She nudged Arn. "Unbelievable as it may seem, you better mark her on the suspect list. Not a prime suspect, but there's a possibility."

16

Arn stopped by Gene's Brickworks, but his secretary said he was out of town on business. He would be back in town that afternoon, and Arn secured an appointment before heading home.

Even before he opened the door, he heard a skill saw shrieking loudly from somewhere in the house. Sawdust made odd-shaped dust motes illuminated by the sun coming in the east window Danny had installed last week. Arn hung up his Stetson, hoping it wouldn't get dusty, before he followed the sound of the saw. Danny stood hunched over two sawhorses in the spare room, his sawing guide clamped to a sheet of expensive-looking knotty pine paneling. "Did I buy that?" Arn asked.

Danny paid him no mind until he finished his cut and stood, arching his back. "What'd you say?"

"That piece of paneling—did I buy that?"

"I put it on your Home Depot account. Why?"

"It looks pricey."

"It was," Danny said as he took out his ear plugs. "But you want this room to look like a quality room, don't you? I keep telling you, Arn, you can't cheap out on quality."

"I just hope I can make my account payment this month."

"You can if you get a paying PI gig instead of looking for Josie Dexter's killer *pro bono*. But I bet you can't quit now."

"Wish I could."

Danny nudged him. "It's the anticipation of finding the killer that's a… drug for you. You get high just thinking about putting bad guys away, even after all these years of being out of the police business. Like sex—the anticipation is so much more exciting that the actual act, even though it's exhausting for you. As I remember sex, that is." He laughed. "Am I right?"

Arn nodded instinctively. Danny was right—for Arn, there was no better drug in life than putting hard criminals behind bars. Or in some cemetery.

He ran his fingers through his hair and motioned to the kitchen.

"I need a break anyway," Danny said and followed Arn into the kitchen. "Since you got that hound-dog look, I'll brew something special this morning."

Arn plopped onto a kitchen chair and rested his arms on the table. "As long as it's something to perk me up, 'cause you're right—this Josie Dexter case has me stumped and worn down. Just like when I was handed the cold case that first day in Robbery-Homicide."

"This will perk you up all right." Danny turned up the burner under the water pot until it whistled. He scooped coffee grounds into a small, tin pot and poured boiling water onto the grounds before capping the lid and letting it sit. "Don't watch it—that's bad luck."

"Don't watch what?"

"The coffee slowly dripping through the grounds. Bad luck. At least, that's what a *mamasan* told me in Vietnam when I first had this."

"Afraid to ask what it is."

"Vietnamese coffee," Danny answered. "You might say I got hooked on it in 'Nam. Starts with Robusta coffee, with the very best coming from Vietnam. It's just that it's a pain to fix, so I only make it for special occasions. And you look like you are a special occasion."

"Does it show?"

"It does." Danny cracked an egg before grabbing the whisk hanging from a hook on the wall and beating it.

"I went to talk with Gene Woods this morning, but he's out of town—"

"See! I told you he was a suspect." Danny added Carnation milk to the egg and beat it frothy with the whisk. "Eddie Bragg's body is not even cold, and now we learn that Gene is out of town. That's gotta mean something for our suspect list."

"All it means is that he's out of town on some business." Arn heard himself defending Gene. For some reason. "Don't mean that he's a suspect at all."

"No?" Danny said. "I met Gene a few years ago. He was laying a basement at a new home in Saddle Ridge. He tossed three bags of mortar on his shoulders like it was three bags of cotton candy you get at Frontier Days before ambling to a pile of bricks. Ambling! And ever notice his hands? His fingers are like thick sausages. I'm telling you, Gene could snap the neck of any man, including little guys like Happ St. John and Eddie Bragg, in case you hadn't noticed."

"That's the problem, I have noticed. You're right—Gene would have no trouble breaking a strong man apart let alone two... anemic guys like Happ and Eddie. Guess that's what's bugging me about Gene—it'd be *too* easy for him to strangle them."

Danny poured the egg and milk mixture into a large, clear mug before slowly—almost lovingly—pouring the brewed coffee into it, the richness combining into... "*Voilà*. Vietnamese coffee."

Arn looked skeptically at it before Danny prodded him. "Go on. Have you ever known me to feed you something that wasn't special?"

"Got a point there." Arn sipped ever so lightly before closing his eyes and sipping more. "My God, that's good."

"Calm you down just a little?"

Arn opened his eyes. "It will. Thanks. I needed something to give me some direction, as this Josie Dexter case is going nowhere." He put the mug down and wiped milk off his upper lip. "Problem with it is there are just *too many* suspects. Every damn person we wrote on the white wall had the opportunity and the motive to kill Happ and Eddie Bragg. And some had the opportunity to kill Josie back in the day."

"Have you talked with Detective Bass again? You know, we could make another trip down to Denver to speak with him."

Arn sipped again and chuckled. "You just want to go down there with me and make a side trip to Sammy's Club."

Danny turned away. "It never crossed my mind."

"Whatever," Arn said. "But I'm not going down there to touch base with The Ass—all the Vietnamese coffee in the world could not get that bad taste out of my mouth. I can call Roger Heinz, though."

Arn took his coffee into the TV room where Danny's remodeling noise would be diminished and dialed Detective Heinz. He picked up on the first ring, and Arn could hear a deep sigh over the phone when Arn asked if Heinz had any updates on Josie Dexter's cold case.

"Nothing. I brought in the guys still alive who attended that bachelor party for reinterviews again, in case they might have remembered something. Anything. But, nope. Nothing."

"All the guys at the bachelor party except Gene Woods," Arn said.

"I might drive up there one more time. I'm really at an impasse with Josie's case. If I don't produce something new soon, the Chief of Detectives will take the case away and order me to work on another cold one."

"Any suspects in that case?"

"It's Sal Bass's case, and he's not exactly forthcoming with information, but when I talked with him this morning, he had absolutely no suspects."

"And by tomorrow The Ass will have moved onto another case."

"'Fraid that's the nature of our business," Heinz said. "If you can't develop anything in the first forty-eight hours, you move on to the next. Unless there's extenuating circumstances."

"Those circumstances being if the victim were prominent in the community," Arn said. "Maybe a politician or his mistress. Someone besides a drunk staggering along East Colfax with a bottle of Thunderbird in his paper sack."

"Guilty again," Detective Heinz said. "On the plus side, there must be some renewed interest in Josie's murder."

"Renewed interest? How so?"

"Some amateur detective stopped by my office and wanted copies of the interviews."

"The TV station's covering of the cold case has generated interest. That's good. Maybe someone will come across something we all missed." Arn finished his Vietnamese coffee and debated whether he should interrupt Danny's remodeling project for another when he dismissed it. "Did you give him copies of the interviews?"

"Had to. Public record. And it wasn't a *he*. It was some frumpy-looking woman who moved like she had rocks in her jeans."

Arn set aside the cup, a sinking feeling replacing his elation at drinking Danny's concoction. "Did the woman give a name?"

Paper rustled on the other end of the line before Detective Heinz said, "Jenessa Wells. Odd name, Jenessa. Just like Josie Dexter's little girl she left orphaned."

Arn took deep breaths. When he and Danny and Ana Maria had tossed around possible suspects in Eddie and Happ's murder, Jenessa's name came to him reluctantly. Now, he wasn't so sure. "Tell me," Arn asked, "did these interview forms contain the addresses of those guys who were at the party?"

"Just their addresses thirty years ago," Heinz answered. "I didn't give her current information about the interviewees. Why?"

Arn explained that it *was* Josie's daughter who had sweet-talked Heinz into giving her police interviews about suspects

119

in her mother's death. And that Jenessa was a Cheyenne PD detective. "Were I you, I would put a watch on the remaining witnesses from that bachelor party."

Heinz laughed nervously. "Surely, you don't think a police officer would hunt up those men. Those addresses are thirty years old. I can tell you from running them down for the reinterviews that they have all moved to other places. She'd play hell trying to find them."

"More like she would play hell on the department computer," Arn said. "Who better to research the witnesses' current addresses than a LEO? I'll keep you posted if I find Jenessa."

17

Arn stopped at the police department and asked the desk officer if Detective Wells was in. "She breezed by here this morning," Greg Smith said. "You coulda played checkers on her coat tails, she ran by so fast. Didn't even say 'howdy' like she usually does. Heard she headed up to her office."

Arn nodded to the computer terminal on the desk next to Smith. "Do you have to sign in with an identification number if you want to access the police databases?"

"I do," Smith said, "but I would get fired if anyone caught me getting into confidential databases for a civilian. Even one who's a former brother in blue."

"I don't want you to. I just want you to go in and see if Detective Wells signed into those databases this morning."

"What's in it for me?"

"The usual," Arn answered. "Triple latte."

Smith glanced at the older man reading, waiting for someone to walk in needing a VIN check. "Could you double check Arn's 442?" Smith asked him.

"What?"

"His VIN number. The insurance company needs it verified."

The man stood and grabbed his cane as he shuffled around the corner of the counter.

"It's parked at the curb," Arn said and watched even as Officer Smith hurriedly turned to his terminal and punched keys. "No sense having a witness."

"I'm with you," Arn answered.

After a few moments, Smith signed off and looked past Arn at the VIN-check civilian donning his glasses and looking through the Oldsmobile's windshield at the vehicle identification number. "Detective Wells was signed into her computer for an hour and forty minutes, but she's not here now. I just sent another investigator a message, and he said she took off after she closed out her computer."

"Isn't she supposed to be working?" Arn asked.

"She took a personal day. Good luck finding her. She skies out of town on her days off to parts unknown."

But known to Arn. He would check later if "Flambé" was headlining Sammy's Club tonight.

*   *   *

When Arn pulled to the curb in front of Maddy's Place, he saw her through the window standing beside a man. He was stripped to his T-shirt as Maddy measured him, presumably for a tailored suit. Arn did not wish Maddy to tip Jenessa off that he was looking for her, and he drove away without talking with Maddy.

He drove to her house and parked beside a grove of aspen across from her home. He dug out his spotting scope and screwed the mount to the side window as he turned his car so he could better scan the house. The garage door stood open; Jenessa's Honda was parked beside a riding lawn mower, but no BMW. And Arn was hoping there would be.

He took off the spotting scope, resigned that he would not talk with her today, and drove back to Gene's Brickworks.

When he pulled into the office that was little more than a trailer, the only thing not coated with a thin film of mortar dust was Gene's bib overalls. He rose from his desk and walked around the corner to offer his hand. "Jasmine said you'd stopped by. Had to make some last-minute checks at a couple jobs before the state inspector comes by. I'm betting this visit is because of Eddie Bragg."

"Know about his murder?"

Gene nodded and shook out a Chesterfield. He offered Arn a cigarette, but Arn waved it away as he dug into his pocket for his pack of Juicy Fruit. "Gave up smoking some time ago, but I still crave one. All it would take is one puff…"

"Then maybe I'd better not—"

"No, go ahead," Arn said. "I can handle it with this," and he tossed the gum wrapper in the round file beside the desk.

"I'll bet," Gene said, "this visit isn't about Smoker's Anonymous lecturing me?"

"I won't lecture you. Takes a strong person to hasten terminal disease."

"Thanks. I think."

"Instead, you can tell me, when was the last time you spoke with Eddie Bragg?"

Gene lit his cigarette with a bent Zippo, a Navy cruiser embossed on the front. He watched smoke rings rising up to be dissipated—like the dust—by the ceiling fan. Stalling. "I haven't seen Eddie for nigh on twenty years, except for a couple years ago. I ran into him panhandling outside the stadium in Denver as I was going in for a Rockies' game. Didn't hardly recognize him, all frail-looking, like he hadn't eaten in weeks. He was always a little feller, but nothing like what I saw that day. I gave him a few bucks to presumably buy supper, and that was it. Shame someone killed him, and for what? I doubt he had much on him."

"Sounds like he went downhill from when you and Haven Talish and Happ St. John hung around?"

"Big time," Gene answered. "He always liked his hooch, but he was never a drunk."

"What do you suppose happened that he let himself go like he did?"

Gene snubbed out his cigarette in an ashtray in the shape of a miniature tire, only half-smoked. Stalling again, Arn thought. "What happens to some men to cause them to go south?"

"Maybe," Arn said, "just maybe, Eddie got worried about Josie Dexter's murder."

Gene shrugged. "No sense to. Eddie was like the rest of us—he was at that party and watched her sashay out the door to go find some work on the street. Eddie was still at the party when that stripper left."

"But he left with Happ St. John, following her, and was probably the one who helped Happ stuff Josie into that dumpster." Arn explained that Happ's blood was definitely on the dumpster. "Maybe Eddie Brag was that other man. Maybe that's what caused him to turn to the bottle to forget."

"Heard that, too," Gene said. "Denver news said the cold case detective had a positive match on that blood at the dumpster where they found her." Gene said. "But Eddie? He got queasy when he found there was even going to be a naked woman at the party." Gene walked around his desk and brushed the dust off before dropping into his chair. "You might not believe this, but Eddie never had a mean bone in his body. He was shy, too. We had to trick him into coming to the party where a stripper was to perform, he was so... reserved."

The flavor had run out of his chewing gum, but Arn would wait until he left the office to shuck it. "Tell me what you remember about that bachelor party?"

Gene forced a laugh. "I would bet you have copies of the interviews we all gave to the investigators. Even the one that Detective Heinz did when he came down here to talk with me a few weeks ago."

Arn nodded. "I have them, but when a person speaks it from memory, sometimes they recall something they had forgotten previously."

"I don't see—"

"Humor an old, retired cop," Arn said.

Gene sat back and explained to Arn almost *exactly* what he had told Neal Barton at the time, and what he had told Roger Heinz when he drove up here from Denver a few weeks ago. Sounding almost exactly like what Happ and Eddie had told Heinz when he brought them in again before their deaths. Three of the Four Amigos—as Gene called them because

Haven was out of town at a football game—were invited to a bachelor party for one of their friends. The three arrived to find seven others already there. A keg of Coors sat in the middle of the room. The keg were running dry when... a lithe woman stepped from a side room wearing little more than frilly panties and a wide smile. The party goers started getting rowdy, but it was civil with nothing inappropriate going on, until the woman stopped dancing and announced she had other commitments before abruptly leaving. "After it came out that Happ St. John was one of the men who carried the dead hooker to the dumpster, it dawned on me that he *had* followed her out of the party," Gene said.

"Who was the other one who followed her out?" Arn asked. "The man who helped Happ?"

"I don't recall anyone else."

Gene looked away and his fingers tapped nervously on his desk. "I really can't tell you anything more. Now, if there's nothing else, I have to get back to the job site."

Arn started for the door when he turned on his heels and walked back to Gene, Columbo-style. "There is one other thing... the tontine. That investment scheme you had with your *Four Amigos. Two* Amigos now that Happ and Eddie Bragg are dead. That leaves the plan to be divided between you and Haven Talish."

"It does," Gene said.

"Unless some tragedy happens to you."

"How's that?"

"The investment plan allows the last survivor to cash in the policy in the unlikely event that three of the four members die. The *unlikely* part already happened with Happ and Eddie's murders. That leaves you and Haven." Arn pasted his broadest Arn-Anderson-grin on his face and said, "Were I you, I'd make sure I double-checked when crossing the street. Lock my doors at night. Make sure that person following me doesn't have bad intentions. I'd hate to see another *unlikely* event happen to another of the Four Amigos."

18

"What the hell? Are you checking up on me? Implying that I might be responsible for their deaths?" Jenessa's crimson face and tightening jaw muscles matched the clenching of her fists as if she were about to attack Arn.

When he had finally found her at home, he first asked why she needed to take a personal day at the last minute.

"I don't appreciate you sticking your nose into my business—"

"...spending nearly two hours on the police computer on your day off. Just what were you researching?"

"None of your damn business," Jenessa said.

"My guess—if we go and look at your computer history— is that you were looking up addresses in Denver. I bet you researched the whereabouts of every man who was at your mother's last bachelor party."

Jenessa looked away, gathering her thoughts. "Sure, I was trying to find out where they lived. How the hell else am I going to interview them?"

"About?

"My mother's last bachelor party, just like you said. Someone knows more than they've told through the years."

Arn popped a piece of gum while he gathered his thoughts. "Let me get this straight... you intend to hunt up everyone on that list and interview them, while numerous interviews through the years have failed to glean any significant information that would solve Josie's murder?"

"You do have a grasp of things," Jenessa said as she leaned back against the wall beside her academy photo and a shadow box with the guns behind thick glass. "So, you got me—I want to find her killer, and he may have attended that party."

"You think one or more of them are hiding something?"

"I do."

"And how will you get them to talk—by strong arming them? Threatening them?"

"You know I'm an investigator with the PD. Through the years, I have developed some pretty impressive interviewing skills."

"You think those skills will force someone to talk after all these years? After being interviewed multiple times by some of the best interrogators?"

Jenessa's face lost its red color. She slowly regained her composure. "I most certainly do. One of those guys who ogled Josie at that bachelor party knows what really happened that night. Now, leave me the hell alone so I can do just that. And I mean it, Anderson—leave me alone, or I'll arrest you for stalking."

*   *   *

Ana Maria cradled her mug of hot cocoa and stared at the white wall. "Guess this just might put Jenessa lower on our suspect list. But I don't see why."

"Because she researched the current addresses of the bachelor attendees thirty years ago, I would elevate her on the list of suspects," Danny said as he tamped tobacco in his pipe with a piece of deer horn. A pipe that looked suspiciously like the one Basil Rathbone always carried in the Sherlock Holmes movies.

"Because she was pissed that you might be accusing her, right?" Ana Maria asked Arn.

"She was livid," Arn replied. "I thought for a moment there that she'd start throwing punches."

"That's another reason why I put her high on the suspect list." Ana Maria walked to the white wall with a green Sharpie in hand. "One of the indications that someone is more likely than not innocent of what they're being accused of is abject indignation. That's the one thing I learned from you."

Arn grinned. "Is that the only thing?"

Ana Maria waved the air with her Sharpie. "You know what I mean. If she was that angry at getting accused—"

"You're not making any sense," Danny said, as he pointed at the wall with his unlit pipe.

"I'm taking into account that Jenessa's a law officer. Any cop worth their salt knows that's just the way an innocent person ought to react—with firm indignation at being accused of a crime they did not commit. She could just as well have put on a show for me, knowing *I* know that's how an innocent person would act when they're falsely accused, even if I just implied it."

"So, she goes up a notch on our suspect list?" Danny asked.

"Wipe your chin."

Arn accepted Danny's dusty shop rag he pulled from his back pocket. He wiped peach filling off his chin and said, "I believe that Jenessa has to be elevated, not based on her reaction—'cause I don't know if her indignation was true or feigned. She floats to the top of the list because she purposely, almost secretly, slipped into the police department on her time off and researched addresses of those men still alive who were interviewed in Josie's murder."

"You know that for certain?"

Arn hesitated. "My PD contact told me that off the record."

"Can you go to the police chief with your suspicions?" Ana Maria asked. "Find out just what she was doing on the computer?"

"I could," Arn said, "if I had something besides mere suspicion. But if I *wrongly* accuse her of stepping over the line—or worse—a good officer's career will be forever ruined."

"If you don't do something," Ana Maria said, "some men's lives may be cut short."

"If we had time and resources, we could surveil her, but that's not going to happen." Arn handed Danny back his dusty shop rag. "I'll call Roger Heinz. Maybe there's something he can do from the Metro end. I'd hate to have any of those other men turn up like Happ or Eddie."

Ana Maria checked her watch and stood abruptly. "Crapola."

"Crapola what?"

"A date. I don't want to be late. I gotta change."

"A date?" Danny said. "You have a date?"

"I do. Dinner at Good Time Charlie's. Don't wait up for me," Ana Maria said as she ran out of the room.

Arn looked up at the ceiling of the spare room under construction and at the fine dust filtering down from her running on the second floor. "Now, who do you suppose she's got a date with?"

Danny gathered up the dishes. "Must be special. Meet you in the TV room—*Survivor* starting in fifteen."

* * *

Sometime between the half-naked babe with the huge mole on her forehead getting voted off the island and the guy claiming to have "jewels" as big as the fake coconuts hanging off the fake tree, Arn drifted off to sleep. In the middle of his nap, the phone rang. When a man identified himself as an intern at the hospital, Arn sat up instantly awake.

"Repeat that," Arn said.

"You are listed as a contact for Ms. Villarreal."

Arn kicked the footrest on the recliner down while he rubbed sleep out of the corners of his eyes. "I don't understand."

"There has been an accident involving Ms. Villarreal, and Arnold Anderson is listed as a contact. You are Arnold Anderson?"

Now, Arn was fully awake and nearly shouted into the phone, "What kind of accident?"

The orderly ignored him and said, "If you come to the Emergency Room, the doctor can explain things," and disconnected.

"What are you yelling like a wild man about?" Danny staggered half-asleep into the TV room.

"Ana Maria," Arn sputtered as he ran out the room. "She's

apparently had an accident and is in the ER."

"Well, don't go without me," Danny said and headed to his own room to change.

On the way to Cheyenne Regional Hospital, they speculated among themselves what kind of accident Ana Maria had been in. She had never wrecked any of her cars that they knew of and could only conclude that whoever her date was tonight had been involved in a wreck with her in his car. "I'll let you out here," Arn said as he stopped in front of the Emergency Room entrance. "Tell the ER people I'll be in soon as I park."

Arn parked the Olds in the darkened hospital parking garage and ran down the hallway to the Emergency Room. Danny stopped him at the desk and said, "The receptionist just told the ER doc that we're here to see Ana Maria."

"What happened?"

Danny nodded to the young doctor emerging from the Emergency Room swinging doors. "We'll soon know."

A man half Arn's age and a third his size whispered to the ER receptionist who pointed to Arn and Danny standing anxiously in the waiting room. He walked to the waiting area and stopped, looking up at Arn. He identified himself and waited for the doctor's headline version. "A patrolman's already been here to take the report—"

"Report of what?"

"Ms. Villarreal was attacked tonight in the parking lot of Good Time Charlie's."

"Attacked how?"

"Strangled," the doctor said. "But she's lucky. Someone found her unconscious in the parking lot and called it in immediately.

AMR was just a block away after another emergency call and transported her here."

Arn started for the emergency room when the Lilliputian doctor took his arm. "I'll let you in to speak with her, but she can't talk much right now as she's pretty hoarse and sore."

"Will she be all right?" Arn asked.

"That's the unusual thing," the doctor said. "In cases of strangulation, a victim's windpipe is most often crushed. With Ms. Villarreal's, her windpipe is fine. I would speculate that within a few hours, she will be able to talk normally. She's very lucky. Have a seat in the waiting room. I'll finalize her care plan, and then she can go home with you."

19

After two of Danny's lemon-and-rum, spiced ginger teas, Ana Maria's eyelids drooped ever so slightly and Arn figured she was calm enough to tell them about what happened to her in the bar-and-grill parking lot. "You didn't get a look at who strangled you?" Arn asked.

Ana Maria kept the ice packs pasted on either side of her throat. "I'd just said goodnight to Shawn—"

"That the knight in shining armor you met on the internet?" Danny asked as he scrunched sideways in his recliner to face her. "Last I recalled, you had big expectations for him."

"Sounded good on 'Dates for You,' but no, no knight there, shining or otherwise. He ended up being more like a court jester when he started talking about his ex-wife."

"Was he the last person you talked to?" Arn asked.

"He was." Ana Maria winced. She pulled the ice packs away and rubbed the sides of her neck. "There wasn't even a goodnight kiss. I quickly figured out that the sooner I got away from that character, the better."

"So, you're in the parking lot," Arn prodded, "and what,

waving goodbye to this Mister Shawn when someone just jumped you from behind and put a choke hold on you?"

"That's pretty much what happened. After that arrogant bastard Shawn had driven off, I was standing in the parking lot, wondering why I hadn't seen the signs earlier of him being a dud." She leaned over and said to Danny, "I'd feel a lot better if I had just a wee bit more rum in my toddy."

"Is there anything at all you recall of your attacker?" Arn asked. "Any impression. Any perfume you might recognize? Was their speech distinctive?"

Ana Maria shook her head. "My impression was that it was some bum off the street. Whoever jumped me stank like they'd just run a marathon. As for voice, my attacker did whisper something." She took another long sip of the tea. "'Back off the Josie Dexter murder. Tell Arn Anderson to do the same.' Then a couple came out of Good Time Charlie's, and the attacker dropped me in the parking lot."

"Did those people give any description?"

She shook her head. "They didn't even see me at first, lying between my car and another next to it, where I'd been attacked. I yelled my best but not much came out."

Danny capped the bottle of rum they kept for special occasions and hid it from Ana Maria. "The ER doc said you were lucky. Said most people who get themselves strangled have their windpipes crushed."

"Unless your attacker doesn't want you dead and just wants you to back off," Arn said. "Why else issue the warning? Your assailant could have killed you."

Ana Maria swirled what was left of her drink around in

her mug before downing the last. She squinted as she eyed the bottom of the mug. "That was just my impression—that my attacker wanted me left alive."

"So, you do have some idea?" Arn asked, anxious for *something* that would lead him to the person he could throttle within an inch of their life before dropping them off at the front door of the county jail.

Ana Maria stood on wobbly legs and quickly plopped back down. "I just think I'll sleep in the recliner, if that's all right with you two."

"Ana Maria," Arn said, resting his hand on her forearm before she fell asleep in the chair, courtesy of the rum toddies Danny had mixed for her. "What caused you to think at the time that killing you was not the attacker's plan?"

Her eyelids drooped as she gathered her thoughts. "Remember that Citizen Police Academy I attended at the Police Department here four years ago?"

Arn chuckled. "The one where you came home and grilled me with questions about police procedure you'd learned?"

"That's the one," Ana Maria answered. "Remember, every night, they covered a different aspect of policing? Well, one night they covered custody and control... managing a combative arrestee. They asked for a volunteer to demonstrate the dreaded choke hold."

"I remember you telling me how you wouldn't be so quick to judge police choke holds after that. What's your point?"

"The point is," she answered slowly, "it *wasn't* a choke hold that officer put on me. It was what the police instructor called a Vascular Neck Restraint. It looks like a choke hold, but the windpipe is not in danger of being crushed. The instructor slid his arm around and applied pressure to both sides of my neck with his arm, my windpipe untouched in that space created by his forearm and elbow."

She rubbed the sides of her neck again. "I think it was someone who knew just how to apply such a move. A wrestler, or maybe someone else who attended a Citizen's Academy."

"Maybe," Danny said, "a policeman."

"Or police*woman*," Arn added.

* * *

Danny pranced nervously back and forth in front of the white wall in the spare room before stopping and examining the notes they had marked there over the past few days. "We have to elevate Jenessa on our suspect list. She was in Denver during the times that both Happ and Eddie were murdered. She all but threatened you today when you finally caught up with her, plus she works out. She's more than strong enough to do that neck restraint thing on Ana Maria. If it's something police are taught, then she would know it."

"Anyone could research it on YouTube," Arn said, "if they wanted to find out how to incapacitate a person in an instant. But Jenessa is obsessed with finding her mother's killer. Though, why would she want Ana Maria and me to back off looking into it? If we uncover something no one else has, it could help solve the case."

Danny paused, pipe in hand as if fending off Arn's objections. "First off, if you continue looking into Josie's death, it might actually lead to the suspect with an arrest and trial afterward. I have a feeling—and it's just a feeling—that Jenessa would rather find Josie's killer herself so she can kill them like she might have killed Happ and Eddie Bragg."

Arn grabbed the carafe of coffee and refilled their cups. "I'm not so sure. What I am sure about is that Happ and Eddie's murders are tied to Josie's death thirty years ago. I'm inclined to believe that, if we find out who killed her, we might find out who killed them."

Arn stood with his cup in hand, staring at the white wall, now not so white with all the columns of suspects marked with the black Sharpie. Other notations in green. Some red. "Gene Wood was at that bachelor party. What if he wasn't telling the truth? What if he followed Happ and Josie out of the party? Happ was a little guy—he'd need help, for certain, carrying Josie's body and hoisting her up and into that dumpster. Gene would have been stout enough to do that."

Danny nodded in agreement. "I can see that. Ana Maria said her attacker smelled like he—or she—just came from a workout, all sweaty. Gene works like a manic laying stone. My guess is that, when he leaves the job site every day, he needs a shower. Badly. And as powerful as he is, Gene could easily overpower Ana Maria."

"Then why not ambush me instead?" Arn said. "She can't even devote much time to the case 'cause she's covering all those other secondary stories DeAngelo wants her to. But me—I have all the time on my hands to pry. To get to the bottom of this. *I* should have been the one choked out. *I* should have been the one warned."

Danny sat in his recliner and rested his hand on Arn's forearm. "I recognize that tone. You're guilting yourself into thinking it should have been you. But don't overthink it. Maybe Ana Maria's attacker ambushed her, knowing she was important to you. Knowing her safety was paramount to you. It wouldn't be the first time she's nearly bought the farm only to have her knight in shining armor save her—you."

Arn had to admit it was true. Ana Maria had a habit of getting herself into dangerous predicaments with her nightly broadcasts that invariably opened old wounds in violent people. Lately, DeAngelo had allowed her to air updates of the murder of Happ St. John, as there was a local connection with his ex-wife. That had blossomed into covering Eddie Bragg's murder, again by strangulation. Arn wondered how she would cover her own assault in Good Time Charlie's parking lot.

He nursed his coffee as he thought about what Danny said. Arn had never had children. Never had anyone that he needed to worry about after Cailee, his wife of twenty-one years, died of cancer a year after he was promoted to detective at Metro. No one. Until he met Ana Maria as she was doing a story when she was with the Denver CBS affiliate. For some reason, he had felt the need to protect her and protect her he did in Denver. He was relieved when she took the job as primary reporter for the TV station here in Cheyenne, a relief that quickly changed to concern as she was constantly getting in over her head, each time cheating death by a hair.

"Another thing is Gene is ex-Navy."

"How's that?"

"Gene was a Seabee. Remember the unidentified circular

bruise on Happ's neck the size of a button? I would bet those Navy peacoats have buttons on the sleeves. Just about the place where an attacker's arm would contact Happ's neck."

"Then you'd lose the bet."

"How?"

"Peacoats," Danny said. "When I was in 'Nam, I saw many a squid wearing peacoats. They had no buttons on the sleeves."

"Well, ain't I the dumbass," Arn said, annoyed at himself for *assuming* Gene may have worn a Navy surplus coat. "But that don't mean he wasn't wearing a coat with buttons."

"And I'll let you off the hook," Danny said, threatening to light his pipe in the house with his Zippo in one hand. "That witness did mention the other guy at the dumpster with Happ had an eagle tat on one upper arm. Might have been something the Seabees got like us grunts."

Arn looked at their notes while Danny remained quiet. The old man had come to recognize when Arn needed to think things through. "One name on that list that ought to be moved higher is Haven Talish."

Danny stood and turned to the white wall once again. He tapped where Arn had originally placed Haven's name, low on the list, but then pointed to where Arn had recently moved it higher. "You moved him there because he's one of the last two to benefit financially from the tontine with Eddie and Happ's deaths, I would bet. If Gene Woods dies next, Haven will inherit the entire amount. And several thousand bucks gathering interest all these years will be significant."

"There's another reason."

"What?"

141

"Grab me another piece of your peach pie and I'll tell you."

"What, I'm your indentured servant now?"

"So, report me. The pie?"

While Danny retreated to the kitchen, Arn thought about Haven Talish and his probable run for governor. That alone should have landed him last on the suspect list, for the last thing he would want is to be associated with a group who'd partied hearty thirty years ago and might be connected to a prostitute's death. Then there was the tontine investment scheme that Haven would benefit from with Eddie and Happ's deaths. Arn thought back to the last time he had been in Haven's office admiring the sports memorabilia adorning the walls. He had the overwhelming feeling that something wasn't quite right and he had researched Haven...

"Here's your pie," Danny said and set a plate with just a sliver on the plywood across the sawhorses.

"That's not enough to feed a sparrow," Arn said, eyeing Danny's piece that was three times as big. "Look at yours."

"And look at you. I don't need to watch my calories. You, on the other hand, my big friend..." he trailed off. "Just tell me why the devil Haven ought to be any higher than he was a few days ago?"

Arn took two bites and his pie was gone. He turned and faced the white wall while he wiped his mouth with a rag hanging by a nail off the plywood. "When I was talking with Haven in his office, I saw that the walls are lined with sports memorabilia. All sorts of sports memorabilia."

"You said he was a Philadelphia sports fanatic as he's from Philly."

"But there was that one piece of memorabilia that just seemed... off. That October 2nd game in '94 when Philadelphia beat the 49ers at Candlestick Park."

"What was off about it?"

"What bugged the hell out of me afterwards was why would a person hang that particular ticket under archival glass? A ticket dated the exact day that Josie Dexter was murdered. So, I got to checking and remembered what Haven told me about it. He said Philadelphia 'tweaked by' the 49ers for the win. Now, I used to follow football, though neither San Francisco nor Philadelphia was my team. I recall one game back then when Philadelphia ran roughshod over San Francisco in a forty-one to eight defeat and checked the date. It was the same date on the game ticket hanging on his wall."

Danny devoured the last bite of his pie and said, "Guess you'll just have to visit with the future governor again."

"Just my thought," Arn said. "Soon as I polish off another piece of pie."

"Maybe I should go with you." Ana Maria stood in the doorway for a moment before sitting in front of the white wall. "There might be an angle there with Haven a possible future governor," she said, her voice still hoarse.

"I heard you banging away in the computer room," Arn said. "You think you're up to going out right now? It's only been since last night that you were attacked."

"I called DeAngelo and he said take as much time off as I need to get over it. So, I put my 'free' time to good use and came away thinking Haven Talish needs to be in the spotlight."

"You, too? Why is that?" Danny asked.

"I got an anonymous tip on my voicemail sometime last night," she said. "Someone thinks I should look into Haven's finances."

"An anonymous tip as in an opponent?" Arn asked.

"Be my guess," Ana Maria answered. "So, I got to digging into Talish Industries. Our future governor—if he can drum up enough money to campaign on 'cause he doesn't have much of his own—is just getting by by the skin of his perfect pearlies."

"You sure?" Danny asked. "Talish Industries is the biggest employer of blue-collar workers in southeast Wyoming. Gas and oil. He's got his hands into—"

"Into so many things," Ana Maria interrupted, "but hasn't profited from any of them. He's strung four banks along with notes that are due this fall, and he is close to filing Chapter Eleven."

Arn thought back to the opulence of Haven's office building, the photos lining the walls of the waiting room: oil rigs working; gas lines being tapped; pipe being laid all to extract wealth from Talish wells. He also thought how a man in financial trouble might benefit from the members of his tontine dying off. "I've tried making appointments to talk with Haven even before your research and after I looked up that football game that is the too-perfect alibi, but his secretary keeps putting me off. You couldn't corner that man in a round room. Short of staking out his parking lot, we'll play hell getting an interview with him."

Ana Maria smiled. "Do you know what a man running for high office needs the most? Publicity. The priceless kind one gets from having their mug plastered on television. I'll call and land an interview. He just doesn't need to know you'll be along with your own questions for him."

"You plan to ambush him about his finances, I would imagine?" Arn asked.

"Let's say we will see where the interview leads us." She stood and said over her shoulder as she left the room, "Give me twenty minutes and I'll have that man cornered in that round room."

20

Arn pulled into a parking spot at the far end of Talish Industries and rocked his car back and forth until it snapped out of second gear and he could turn it off. Against Ana Maria's objections, he had once again crawled under his car in the backyard to work on the shift linkage, and once again, seemed to make it worse off than before.

"I told you," she said, "it's just a matter of time before the linkage locks up all together. Then you'll be stuck in traffic climbing underneath to free it. I told you I'd fix it when I got the chance."

"But I need a car to get around."

"You could have taken that car the neighbor kid gave you."

"That's not a car—it's a Yugo, and I am *not* driving that." The neighbor's son next door had just graduated high school and enlisted in the Air Force. "I can't take it with me, Mr. Anderson. Here's the title."

"Why not leave it until you graduate basic training and take it to your base?"

"For one," the kid said, "it wouldn't make it much farther

than the city limits. Second, military bases require insurance on vehicles. Do you see any insurance company covering that?"

"Then leave it with your dad."

The kid chuckled. "He won't be caught dead having that in his yard one minute longer."

"But you think I would?"

The kid shrugged as he nodded to Arn's Oldsmobile. "You already have junk sitting around."

Before Arn could hand the title back, the kid turned on his heels and *ran* back to his house, leaving Arn with the car that he wasn't even sure would make it into the backyard. Arn promptly parked it in back where no one could see it. He had contemplated filling it with topsoil, planting ferns and foliage, making it into a gigantic terrarium.

"Suit yourself," Ana Maria said, "but mark my word, one of these days, this linkage is going to get so jammed up, I'm going to have to replace the whole system."

Arn followed Ana Maria past an outside Talish Industries display of a mini pumpjack slowly bobbing its iron head up and down like an exhausted gooney bird. When they reached the front doors, Arn stopped and leaned against the side of the building. He and Ana Maria had worked out a plan whereby she would announce to Haven's receptionist that she was here for their interview. Arn would give her a few moments before entering. Haven—slick though he was at dodging Arn—would be caught flatfooted. Already a practiced politician.

Arn cupped his hand to his ear, the receptionist's faint voice friendly when she greeted Ana Maria as she walked inside. After all, the receptionist's boss was about to get some free advertising in his run for governor. When Arn heard Haven's voice booming over his receptionist to welcome Ana Maria, Arn stepped into the office. It took but a heartbeat for Haven to realize Arn was there, and the genuine smile left Haven's face, replaced by that look many awkward politicians have when caught unawares. "Anderson," he tried sounding as friendly as possible. "Did you follow Ms. Villarreal in here?"

"How else was I to get past that watchdog of a receptionist?" Arn motioned to the glaring receptionist. "Did she *ever* give you my messages that I wanted to talk to you again?"

Haven's jaw muscles tightened. He continued staring at Arn with a forced smile, through his eyes and the rest of his face showed he was far from pleased. "Something must have gotten lost in the translation. Don't you think, Emily?"

The receptionist scowled at Arn. "I must have misplaced the messages. It won't happen again."

"Good." Haven turned to Arn. "Just make an appointment—"

"We might as well visit now."

"What Arn talks with you about might be of interest to my listeners," Ana Maria said in her most treacle voice. "Anything to help your campaign get traction."

"I doubt if anything Anderson says will be of any help, but you both might as well step into my office. By the way, Ms. Villarreal, where is your cameraman?"

"This is a preliminary interview" Ana Maria lied. "As soon as we figure out how long you should be on-air, I will arrange a full photo shoot with my cameraman."

"Fair enough." Haven held the door for Ana Maria and paused before doing the same for Arn. "Thank you, Governor," Arn said in a soft voice that might have even rivaled Ana Maria's come-hither voice.

Haven motioned to overstuffed leather chairs, the arms made of steer horns, the feet fabricated from the hooves of cows, the Talish Industries pumpjack logo embossed on the chair backs that Arn speculated cost more than he made a month in retirement. When he had seen them when he was last in the office, Arn figured it was pocket change for Haven. Now with Ana Maria's research about Haven being strapped for cash, and about filing for bankruptcy protection, Arn realized that Haven overspent. Haven had propped his personal and professional image up to keep them looking like one of the state's premier energy development companies.

Haven sat on the edge of his desk and said, "No recorder?"

"This initial interview is off the record so we can talk about whatever we like. Then we can determine where I want to focus my broadcast." Ana Maria learned from Arn some time ago that people often spoke more freely when they knew they were not being recorded, so she left her micro recorder in her purse.

Haven leaned against his enormous desk and turned so that his back was to Arn. "Where do you want to start?" he asked Ana Maria.

"How about the history of the company and your successes?"

Arn and Ana Maria had talked about Haven's background, having moved to Wyoming shortly after Josie Dexter's murder, so Ana Maria was well-versed in Haven's background. Arn recognized her common tactic of letting people brag about themselves to lower their guard before asking the tough questions. *Damn, she's good*, he thought.

After Haven told Ana Maria much of what was printed on his campaign fliers, he said, "Now that you know basically my life history, what questions do you have?"

She leaned back and rested her forearms on the steer-horns. "Your success that you talk about… I have questions. This is a little sensitive."

"What is?" Haven asked.

Ana Maria cleared her throat. "I understand that you have initiated paperwork to file Chapter Eleven with the bankruptcy court."

"How did you obtain that pearl of information—from one of the six people running against me, no doubt?"

"Let us just say that it is public information—"

"I know it is!" Haven snapped, his tanned face becoming red. He stood and sat behind his desk as if it offered protection from any allegations Ana Maria might throw at him. "Do you intend to make it public?"

"Mr. Talish," Ana Maria said, "all I want to find out is if Talish Industries is directly connected with your campaign—"

"My attorney has filed all the executory contracts—"

"But is it campaign connected?" Ana Maria pressed.

Haven looked away. "I have personal assets the courts can't touch that I am using for my campaign."

"Yet you are strapped?"

Haven leaned his elbows on his desk. "If you put it like that, yes, I am strapped. In case you haven't been following the economy, the oil and gas industry has taken a big hit. And the refinery here quit processing crude a few years ago."

"But you will recover quite nicely when your investment

plan—the tontine you made with your friends while living in Denver—comes due."

"It has not *matured* yet," Haven sputtered. "You forget, Gene Woods is also in the tontine. We'll both profit when it matures in a four more years—"

"Unless Gene winds up dead like Happ St. John and Eddie Bragg," Arn said.

"I don't think I like your tone," Haven said. He stood and leaned over his desk. Though shorter and not as heavy as Arn, he would still be a handful if he leapt across his desk.

He turned to Ana Maria. "Is this why you brought Anderson along—to make accusations?"

She shrugged. "You have to admit that the look is bad—two of the four tontine members murdered at the same time that you're having financial difficulties. Don't you know people want transparency from their gubernatorial candidates?"

Haven nodded to the door. "I think this interview is finished."

Ana Maria and Arn stood and headed for the door when he paused at the wall where Haven displayed his Philadelphia football memorabilia. "This is actually the reason I wanted to talk with you," he said and pointed to the ticket stub for the Eagles victory over New England. "I admired Philadelphia that season."

Haven's eyes darted to the ticket stub enshrined under archival glass. "I didn't know you were an Eagles fan."

"Let's say I followed them that season. I was especially excited during that game with Brister as QB. His passing game wasn't up to snuff, making it such a tweaker."

Haven's facial muscles relaxed as if relieved by talking with a fellow fan. "His fumbles made that a close game, no doubt."

"Except it wasn't close, not with a 41-8 score," Arn said. "And Brister wasn't quarterback—Randall Cunningham was."

Haven's shoulders slumped and he backed up a step until he could rest against his desk for support. "How do you know—"

"It's called the internet," Arn said. "I looked it up. That game was one of the worst defeats in 49er history. The other day when I was here, that date stood out in my mind, for some reason. After I left, I wracked my brain, trying to figure out why you displayed a stub from a game that you clearly didn't watch. Then it hit me, and I just knew."

Haven's voice faltered when he said, "Knew what?"

Arn tapped the frame. "*That* is your bona fide that you were not in Denver the day Josie Dexter was murdered. You hung that up so folks thought you were out of town at the time of the murder, in case it ever came up."

"Is that true?" Ana Maria pressed, knowing it was. "Would you care to tell us why you have been pushing the narrative all these years that you were not in Denver when Josie was killed?"

Haven used the desk for support as he walked behind it on shaky legs. He plopped down into his chair and reached into a mini-fridge beside his desk. He withdrew a bottle of Perrier and downed half of it before capping it and setting it aside. "How much do you know... Is this off the record? This doesn't have to be made public, does it?"

"Off the record as far as I'm concerned," Arn said. "Ana Maria?"

"Off the record here, too."

Haven polished off the last of his water and dropped it into the round file beside his desk. "What is it you want to know?"

"About that night Josie was murdered."

"How much do you know?" Haven asked.

"I talked with Gene Woods," Arn answered, leaving the implication that Gene had said something about Haven and the night of Josie's death that was a secret between the two men.

Haven took a deep, calming breath. "Josie Dexter. Do you know how many years I agonized about her?"

"Agonized how?" Arn asked.

"Guilt. Of the highest order." He looked at his fridge as if he needed another bottle of water to calm himself. "As I suspect Gene's told you, that bachelor party wasn't Josie's last gig."

Arn and Ana Maria sat silent, waiting for Haven to unburden himself.

"Happ called me up that night as the bachelor party was winding down."

"For my curiosity," Ana Maria said, "you were not at that party with the rest of your friends?"

Haven shook his head. "I had a migraine and begged off, so, no, I was not there."

"But at some point, you did party with Josie?"

"Happ called and woke me up. 'We got a hot babe here and she's affordable,' he said. 'But we need a place where we can have a private party.' So Happ and Gene and Eddie brought Josie over to my place to party."

"Why your place?" Ana Maria asked, putting up her hands. "Off the record."

"I was the only single guy in our bunch. The rest wanted a good time, but Lord knows, there would have been hell to pay if their wives found out."

Arn popped a piece of Juicy Fruit and offered Haven one, but he waved it away. "Tell us what happened when Josie left your place?"

"She left with Happ and Eddie," Haven said, "after we all... had our turn with her."

"Guess your migraine wasn't as bad as you said," Arn said.

"Once I got a look at her, you might say the migraine subsided."

"When she left your place..." Arn pressed.

Haven shrugged. "After she left, I can't say, except later—when she was found dead in the dumpster—we all swore we'd never talk about that night. Now with Happ being a positive match to one of the men who stuffed her in that dumpster, I can only conclude Eddie was the other man with Happ."

"Except he wasn't," Arn said. "The witness on the second-floor landing clearly saw the sleeve rolled up on the other man with Happ. And on his arm was an eagle tattoo that Eddie Bragg never had. A military tat. Your campaign brochure says you served in the National Guard here in Wyoming."

"If you're suggesting I have such a tattoo on my arm, you've got it wrong."

"For now," Arn said, "I'll take your word for it. Which means Happ St. John's accomplice who helped him dispose of Josie Dexter's body is still out there."

Arn stretched his back. "Which brings us to why anyone would want to kill Eddie Bragg unless the killer didn't want to be found out about that night."

"Are you accusing me?" Haven said, though there was little conviction in his voice, as if he knew his fate was in the hands of Arn and Ana Maria.

"You got to admit," Arn said, "you're at the top of the suspect list. First off, Eddie and Happ could have dimed you out about the night Josie Dexter was murdered, even if you didn't have anything to do with it. Be bad in the middle of a gubernatorial campaign for people to hear you went through this elaborate scheme just to set up an alibi for that night," Arn tapped the ticket stub. "Secondly, as Ana Maria pointed out, you're financially strapped. With Eddie and Happ gone… well, you see where this is headed?"

"You both said this is all off the record?"

Arn looked at Ana Maria and she nodded. "It is," Arn said, "under the condition that you contact Detective Roger Heinz with the Cold Case Unit in Denver. I think he'll be interested in what you have to say."

"But I don't know anything that would help him."

"Knowing Josie was alive when Happ, Eddie, and Gene brought her to your house would help. Knowing Happ and Eddie both left your place with Josie would alter the timeline."

Haven dropped his head. "All right. I will call the investigator this afternoon. But please don't let any of this out."

They started out of Haven's office when Ana Maria stopped and faced him. "Where were you last night around nine o'clock?"

"I was… with a lady. Why, do I need an alibi for last night, too?"

"Maybe," Ana Maria answered. "Who was the lady?"

"That," Haven said, "is strictly personal. I am not going to involve someone else in my foolish mistakes. But again, why do I need an alibi for last night?"

Ana Maria pulled back her cowl-neck sweater to show Haven

the bruises on her neck. "Someone choked me in the parking lot of Good Time Charlie's last night."

"And you think it was me? Well, you can damn well look someplace else. Until you have some kind of proof that I am your culprit, I am not telling you who I was with when," he nodded to Ana Maria's bruises, "that happened."

21

"From what you just told me," Danny said, "Haven not only could have been Happ and Eddie's killer but also the one who attacked Ana Maria. The man's darn well big enough."

He was, Arn had to admit. Choking out a woman—even a stout lady like Ana Maria—would have been an easy thing for Haven. But... "I just don't know if he would risk that. His face has been plastered all over the newspaper in campaign ads, and his volunteers have been handing out his fliers all across town. Anyone leaving Good Time Charlie's could recognize him." He turned to Ana Maria. "Did you get any vibes when we were in Haven's office that he was your attacker?"

Ana Maria set her empty ice cream bowl on the TV tray and dabbed at her mouth with a napkin. "Can't say, but then the choking happened so fast. I felt almost immediately that I was passing out when that arm snaked around my throat. But a few hours ago talking with Haven, I got no inclination he was lying when he said he was with a woman."

"Why all the secrecy?" Danny asked. "If he told you her name, his alibi would be easy to verify."

"Perhaps his lady friend is someone he doesn't want the public to know about," Ana Maria said. She kicked the footrest on her recliner back and draped a blanket over her feet and legs. "Maybe she's married. Or maybe Haven just doesn't want his persona of the unattached bachelor being tarnished. After all, if he's elected governor, there might be a First Lady in the wings."

Danny drew an arrow moving Haven to the top of the suspect list beside Jenessa. He stepped back and declared, "We have us a real horse race here."

"Can't argue there." Arn stood beside Danny at the white wall with all the scribbling staring back like it was a frozen movie screen. "A moment before we stepped into Haven Talish's office this afternoon, I knew—just *knew*—Jenessa was our prime suspect. As obsessed as she is with her mother's murder, I know she wants justice. I envisioned her rationalizing killing Happ and Eddie if she thought they were the ones who stuffed her mother's body in the dumpster. Now, I'm not so sure, with the great lengths Haven went to convince people he was not in Denver the night Josie was murdered."

"Too bad you don't know who he claims to have been with last night when Ana Maria was attacked," Danny said. "That's if there even *is* a woman who can vouch for him."

"Oh, there's a woman, all right," Arn said.

"How can you be sure of that?" Danny asked.

Arn motioned to Ana Maria relaxing in her recliner. "Because *she* believed Haven when he said he was with a woman last night. And you know how I trust women's intuition. Saved my bacon more than once working the street with a woman officer."

"Still doesn't do anything to find her."

Arn bent over and pulled his cowboy boots on. "No? Want to go for a ride to keep me company?"

"Sure," Danny said. "Anything to get out of the house. This remodeling is getting old. Where are we going?"

"To a grove of trees east of town," Arn answered. "Right across from Haven Talish's house. For a little surveillance."

Danny groaned. "I was afraid you'd say something like that. I got the feeling that we'll be sitting there a while. I'll brew coffee for the Thermos."

*　*　*

The many years Arn worked the street here in Cheyenne and later with the Denver Police, the one thing he hated the most was surveillance. Boring surveillance. Sitting, watching, waiting for the target to move. To make a mistake. It was that target who now walked out of his house. He looked about, but Arn knew Haven wouldn't spot the Oldsmobile among the trees. Arn nudged Danny awake. "Our boy's on the move."

Danny folded his bony knees under himself and sat upright. He rubbed the sleep out of his eyes and uncapped the Thermos. "That's a relief. I thought we were going to need Domino's delivered here."

Arn wondered the same thing himself. They had been watching Haven's house for nearly six hours now, taking turns dozing, and Arn thought this might have been a silly idea.

He waited until Haven's Cadillac turned the corner of his block before Arn turned on his own headlights and began following. Always following as far behind as possible. Always following as close as he could without being made by the target.

"Where d'you suppose he's going this time of night?" Danny asked.

Arn checked his watch: one-fifteen. Even the bars would soon be closed, so Haven wasn't headed somewhere for a drink.

Arn had no delusions when he decided to tail Haven. As with all the surveillance he had done in years past, the target might be going no further than the nearest 7-Eleven for milk or cigarettes before heading back home, whereupon Arn would park once again where he could watch. Was Haven going to a convenience store? Arn prayed he wasn't, as he kept Haven's taillights in sight two blocks ahead.

"If he's going to a tap room before last call, he'd better hurry," Danny said.

"From what Ana Maria's learned about Haven, he's not a drinker, so he's gotta be going somewhere else… there."

Haven doused his lights and pulled to the curb.

Arn did the same and slowly eased his car closer, careful not to hit anything parked along the street. What he wouldn't give for a full moon's illumination right now. He used the parking brake to stop without telltale brake lights giving him away.

They waited in the dark for Haven to climb out of his car. Or to pick someone up at this remote spot. "He's gotta be meeting someone," Danny said. "Maybe her." He pointed but Arn could not see who Danny referred to. Even though the man was old by Lakota standards, he retained eyesight that made Arn envious. "She's just standing in the shadow of those pine trees."

Arn grabbed his binoculars and scanned where Danny pointed. Arn finally spotted a solitary person just standing, when… she looked about before walking out of the shadows and into the light: Jenessa!

She walked directly to Haven's Cadillac and the dome light came on momentarily. It stayed on long enough that Arn could see her bend and kiss him before she shut the door. Seconds later, Haven sped off, but Arn remained where he was parked.

"Aren't we going to tail them?"

"We are not," Arn said. "If they're sneaking around, I am sure the next stop will be an out-of-town motel."

"Why don't they just go to Haven's place?" Danny asked. "Not like he's got a wife or anything. They'd be perfectly alone."

"There's only one reason," Arn said. "They want to keep their relationship absolutely secret."

"Because Haven's old enough to be her father?"

"Nowadays, their age difference shouldn't be an issue."

"Then why sneak around?"

Arn stowed his binos back in the case and said, "I'll know when I talk with Jenessa. Perhaps tomorrow, if she makes it into work."

*   *   *

They sat around the table watching Danny carve the ham like they were watching a celebrity chef doing the honors on television. "I gotta know how Jenessa reacted when you confronted her with smooching Haven Talish," Ana Maria asked.

"About how you react when Danny looks over your shoulder when you're on the computer, looking at those dating sites, searching for a new man."

"It's none of his business who my potential dates are!"

"That was Jenessa's reaction," Arn said as he sat waiting in anticipation of another of Danny's gourmet suppers. "When I told her the way she looked the other night at Sammy's Club she could get any man she wanted, she waved it off. 'I don't want just *any* man,' she told me."

"That was it?" Ana Maria said. "She didn't explain herself any better than that?"

Danny finished and took his apron off before putting his carving set in the dishwasher. "Ana Maria's right—for being caught with possibly the next governor, it seems like she should have more to say for herself than that."

"That was her explanation—that she wished to get close to a man of some importance. Someone—a sugar daddy in other words—who could 'keep' her and allow her to retire."

"Retire from stripping, or police work?" Ana Maria asked.

"Both, but she particularly emphasized that she was getting a little old to continue stripping."

Danny set the bowl of mashed potatoes in the middle of the table and sat across from Arn. "If you ask me, she's in her dancing prime. And all the times she's been the headliner at Sammy's Club proves it."

"But for how long?" Arn said. "Besides, she's still afraid her secret will come to light for the chief. Even after I told her I had a come-to-Jesus moment with Ted Ames so he won't rat her out, she's still worried her secret will reach the police administration. Then, sugar daddy or not, her police career would be over."

"That's understandable," Ana Maria said. "I worked my way through college working nights at Hooters, and a lot of ladies were worried that they were getting too far along in years to be showing off their... wares."

"Thought you worked at your pappy's repair shop?" Danny asked.

Ana Maria frowned as if remembering her time at Hooters was less than pleasant. "I worked for my dad on the weekends. But working for family often pays little 'cause they expect to pay you less, if anything. I had to work nights at the restaurant just to afford my college books. Do you know how many bruises I got from guys pinching my keister as I walked by? I can understand where Jenessa's coming from. Did she threaten to arrest you for stalking her again, following her the other night?"

Arn tucked a napkin under his chin, waiting for Danny to say grace. "She did, until I reminded her I was one of the people keeping her secret that she danced in Denver on her days off."

"You blackmailed her?" Ana Maria said.

"If you want to put it like that, yes—I implied I might not be so silent from a jail cell."

"I would bet she blew her top at that."

"She did, but not as bad as when I suggested she might be sidling up to Haven because it was his house in Denver where he and the three amigos partied the night of her mother's murder. I suggested she was trying to get close to Haven to find out the truth of what happened to her mother that night."

"I thought we'd gotten to the truth," Ana Maria said. "That Happ, Eddie, and Gene brought Josie to Haven's house where they all… had their way with her."

"That's only part of the truth," Arn said.

"Then what's the other part?" Danny asked.

"*That*," Arn answered, "is what we need to find out. All I know is that when Haven starts talking about that night, he gets rattled. And it's not just because his apartment was the last place Josie Dexter laid down for money."

22

Ana Maria banged on Arn's bedroom door and yelled, "Get up!"

Arn rolled over, thinking at first he was dreaming when she banged again. "Get the hell up."

He slid his slippers on and cracked the door. "Tell me this isn't an emergency."

"Not for you," she said, "but for Gene Woods."

Arn opened the door and stepped into the hallway just as Danny yelled up from his first-floor bedroom, "Is there a good reason why you two are yelling like wild people?"

"Gene Woods, apparently," Arn answered.

Danny stumbled up the steps and stood on the second-floor landing with his hands on his bony hips. "What about Gene Woods?"

Arn shrugged and turned to Ana Maria. "Damned if I know. She just woke me up because of something about Gene."

"He's been shot," Ana Maria blurted out. "And it's touch and go for him in ICU."

"How d'you know that?" Danny asked.

C. M. Wendelboe

"Got an alert on my phone. I'm meeting my cameraman at the hospital and thought you'd like to come with me."

"Why would I want to do that?" Arn asked.

"I don't know," she answered as she finished buttoning up her jacket. "Maybe because he could come out of it and say something germane to all that we've been working on concerning Josie Dexter and Happ and Eddie's murders."

"I figure the police will be there when and if he comes out of it." Arn buckled his jeans. "Not much I'll be able to add to Gene's statement. If he gives one."

"You always said another set of eyes often helps and another set of ears might hear something altogether different."

Arn looked at his watch. It was just early enough in the morning that he wouldn't get back to sleep anyway. "At least, let me throw a shirt on."

"Call when you're coming home," Danny said, "and I'll whip up something for breakfast."

*   *   *

After Ana Maria had wrapped up her session with her cameraman, she stood in front of the hospital and pocketed her microphone. "That's a wrap, Phil. I'll call you if anything significant happens."

The cameraman screwed on a lens cover and draped the camera over his shoulder before heading to the parking garage.

Ana Maria looked after him and said, "Wish I had more for my broadcast tonight."

"Can't hardly fabricate things," Arn said. "If Gene ever

166

comes out of it and identifies his shooter, you can record that. But it looks like what you got is about it until Officer Ames calls you."

"That's another thing," Ana Maria said, an apologetic tone to her voice. "I didn't mean to give you the bum's rush when I saw Ted Ames walk into the hospital, but I knew you and he have some bad history between you."

Arn waved it away. "If I'd been there when you questioned him, he would have clammed right up. I am sure he's still stinging from my... *suggestion* that he forget about Jenessa's dancing in Denver. It didn't offend me any to wait down the hallway where he couldn't see me until you were finished interviewing him. And just what did he tell you?"

"Let's talk about it over Danny's special omelet," Ana Maria said. "Taping a segment about a gunshot victim always makes me hungry."

They drove the rest of the way home with Ana Maria giving Arn what-for as he jammed gears. "You shift like you're in a race," she said. "I told you I'd get around to fixing that linkage when I had the chance. I've been a bit busy lately. The alternative is you taking it to a mechanic. John Curtis down at Cheyenne Industrial specializes in Oldsmobiles."

"I'll wait for you to repair it. Or figure it out myself."

"You're cheap."

"Frugal."

"*Cheap.*"

"I am living off my police retirement, and you don't see anyone beating down my door, needing a private investigator, do you?"

Ana Maria snapped her fingers. "You have that fine Yugo sitting in the backyard."

"Would you have chanced that Yugo to get us to the hospital to tape that segment?"

"I see your point," Ana Maria said. "But just this once, be careful that you don't bend the linkage any more than it already is."

* * *

Even before they stepped into the kitchen, Arn could smell the aroma of Danny's breakfast he 'threw together.' "Figured you'd be especially hungry, so I made omelets with duck eggs I bought at the farmer's market this week."

"Sounds exotic," Ana Maria said while she stripped off her jacket and hung it on the back of a kitchen chair.

"Let's say it'll loosen your tongue so you can fill me in about the Gene Woods shooting."

Arn was with Danny—he hadn't heard anything Sgt. Ames told Ana Maria while he was hiding down the hall in the hospital, and she had told him nothing on the ride back. Arn figured that Danny would pester her for information, and by waiting until they got home, she'd only have to tell it once.

Danny passed out utensils and sat across from Arn and Ana Maria. "Let's hear it, and I don't want the headline version. I want to hear all the juicy details."

"Not that many details to tell." Ana Maria sliced into her omelet, melted cheese oozing onto her plate. "Sgt. Ames said dispatch received a call from the Depot Plaza parking lot. A couple coming out of the Albany Restaurant heard a gunshot and saw someone running towards the overpass by the railroad tracks. The couple saw Gene Woods slumped against a pickup, leaking blood onto the parking lot asphalt. Lucky for him, the woman is a firefighter and knew enough to stop the bleeding, or Gene wouldn't have made it to Cheyenne Regional. He still might not make it, as critical as his condition is."

"I would bet," Arn said, "that the couple couldn't identify the shooter?"

"No, but they did name the man Gene was having supper with at the Albany—Haven Talish. Like you said, with Haven's face plastered all over town, it was hard for them not to notice him eating with Gene." She wiped egg off her lower lip. "Before you ask, Sgt. Ames and the on-call investigator were headed over to Haven's house right after the hospital. Ames promises to call me in the morning after he talks with him."

Danny checked his watch, an oversized Mickey Mouse that he'd bought forty years ago and still kept perfect time. "Looks like it's too late in the morning to go back to bed, so we can watch *Wheel of Fortune* while we wait for Ted Ames to call you."

* * *

When Danny guessed the *Wheel of Fortune* word after only two letters were revealed, Arn thought it was a rerun they were watching. "You've seen this episode before."

"I have not," he answered. "I just happen to know things."

"We'll wait until the end of the show, and we'll see just when this was aired." Ana Maria sat looking at her own watch as she fidgeted in her recliner.

"Relax," Arn said, sipping coffee and debating in his mind whether Danny was telling the truth about this *Wheel of Fortune* episode. "Sgt. Ames will call when he's got something. For starters, I'm sure he had to wait to rouse Haven, then the time it took to interview him. Maybe he confessed. Maybe he told Ames to pack sand. I've been in both kinds of interviews, and they both take time. Just be thankful the detective on call wasn't Jenessa Wells."

"That would be one major conflict of interest—Jenessa interrogating the man she is romantically involved with." She looked at her watch again.

Arn grinned. "He'll call if he wants another date with you."

Ana Maria pulled back the blinds. The bright sun revealed dust motes flying about, courtesy of Danny's sawing earlier in the spare room. "DeAngelo's gonna have my behind if all I have to air tonight is what little Ames told me at the hospital—" Her cell phone rang, and she jumped. "Quiet, and I'll put it on speaker. It's Sgt. Ames."

Danny muted the television a second before Ames told Ana Maria, "Here's your update—we interviewed Haven Talish at his home. He had nothing to do with Gene Woods' shooting; at least, that's what Detective Davis says after grilling him for about three hours. And before you ask, Davis is a top-notch interrogator."

"How is Gene?" Ana Maria asked.

"Still in an induced coma. Still touch and go. They dug the bullet out this morning—weighed 121 grains."

"Did the ballistics examiner determine what kind of gun?" she asked.

"We'll send it to the DCI examiner, but Davis can't fix the kind of gun. It measured like a 9mm. But also a .38 and a .38 Super."

'What's that?' Ana Maria mouthed silently, but Arn shrugged. He didn't know either.

"For having an intact bullet," she said, "sounds like you guys don't know much."

"That's just it," Ames said, "it wasn't entirely intact. By the trajectory of the bullet, it yawed when it hit Gene's chest. It was heavily deformed, with part of the bullet jacket lost somewhere in the shooting, so our ballistics guy can't determine a true weight."

Arn motioned for Ana Maria to mute her phone. "Ask him about that trajectory part... might give us an indication as to how tall the shooter is."

Ana Maria connected the voice again and asked Ames about that. "The shooter more than likely knelt down and shot upwards," he explained. "Close range shot, as we found powder residue on Gene's shirt, so he definitely faced his attacker. If he ever comes out of it, I'm certain he'll know just who shot him."

"And you are certain Haven knows nothing?" Ana Maria asked.

There was rustling on the other end of the line as if Sgt. Ames flipped pages in a notebook. "He and Gene Woods had a leisurely supper at the Albany. They even had the same entrée—prime rib. They parted upon exiting, with Haven's car parked down the alley, and Gene's in the Depot Plaza parking lot in the opposite direction."

"Did you do a GSR on Haven?" she asked.

"What?" Ames snapped. "You think we're amateurs? Of course, we did a Gun Shot Residue test on Haven, and it came back clean. By the way, are you going to interview me on-air about this shooting?"

"I'll grab my cameraman, and we'll drop by the PD this afternoon. By that time, you may know more."

"Guess I better get a haircut then. Maybe go to that stylist in the mall—"

"You'll look just fine," Ana Maria said. "The broadcast tonight will give you a chance to ask for the public's help in finding Gene's shooter when we go live."

"That was my thought exactly," Ames said a moment before broaching the subject of dinner with Ana Maria, and she abruptly disconnected.

"You could have had dinner paid for by one handsome police sergeant," Danny said.

"I'll have enough trouble fending off that blowhard when I have to meet up with him in person for the pre-shoot tonight. Let's move to the spare room."

They all three grabbed their coffee cups and moved to sit in front of the white wall. Ana Maria grabbed a Sharpie and drew a pistol named 'Gene's murder weapons.' "Kind of premature," Arn said. "Gene's still hanging on."

"He is," she answered, "but this will make it easier, in case he doesn't pull through."

She jotted the diameter of the bullet and the weight from the information Sgt. Ames gave her and said, "We know this is probably a 9mm. Most common round in this country. Carried by most cops. The .38s... they're a little less common."

"But they used to be the most prominent weapon," Danny said. "Every time I got arrested back in the day, the cop was carrying a .38."

"Or .357," Arn said. "I remember those days. Us cops and security guards, armored car guards, used to carry handguns of that caliber."

Ana Maria wrote that under the 9mm notation. "What's with the .38 Super?" she asked. "I've never heard of that."

"Hell if I know," Arn answered. "Never ran into that one."

"But then, you're not as old as me." Danny stood and faced them as if he were educating a jury. ".38 Supers used to be the gun of choice for gangsters. Shot a bullet about the same size as the .38 and the 9mm—little lighter, though—but with a lot more velocity. Almost exclusively in a 1911-design... a big, flat-sided semi-automatic."

"Then why haven't I ever run into one in my law enforcement career?" Arn asked.

"Because," Danny said, drawing out his answer, "nowadays, it's more of a collector's item."

"Now, all we have to do is find a collector willing to fire an antique?"

"I didn't say it was an antique," Danny said. "I said it is a collector's gun. The shooter might have used such a weapon to throw investigators off."

Ana Maria stood staring at the white wall so long, Arn thought she'd fallen asleep on her feet. "Whatcha staring at?"

"Our suspect list," Ana Maria answered. "When I heard about Gene getting shot, the first person I thought of was Haven. Especially since they had just parted ways after supper. He has financial troubles big time, and with Gene dead, he could cash in on that investment scheme the four guys had. But if Ames and crew did a GSR and it came back clean, now I'm not so sure. I'm about to move Haven down a little on our suspect list."

"Don't write him off quite yet."

"And why not?" she asked. "He was clean of gunshot residue—"

"Because he could have cleaned up. Scrubbed his hands thoroughly and changed clothes. Perhaps wore gloves," Danny said, then added, "didn't mean to steal your thunder, Arn."

"*Forensic Files* again?"

Danny nodded. "Last episode."

Arn turned to Ana Maria. "Danny's right, though. Haven could have watched the same episode, or researched on the internet to learn that gunshot residue would be all over his shooting hand. Some particulates might even be on his clothes from firing the gun. By the time Sgt. Ames and Detective Davis located Haven at home and brought him in for questioning, he could have easily cleaned himself up of any residue."

"So you're thinking he might be good for Gene's shooting?" she asked.

"I'll know more as soon as I talk with him."

Ana Maria chuckled. "Good luck with that. The last time you had to sneak around just to get close enough to him to talk. You go prowling around his office, wanting to talk again, and that shark of a receptionist will put the run on you."

"Unless I ambush him someplace else," Arn said, slipping a schedule from his back pocket. "Looks like he has a campaign stop at Little America this afternoon. Fundraising. I think I'll show up just to hear what he has to say and have a… nice, long visit with our future governor."

"I'll grab my cameraman and go with you."

"I'd rather you talk with Maddy. At her house. The last time I talked with her, she was outright hostile. I doubt she'd let me into her house."

"And just what would we talk about?" Ana Maria asked.

Arn shrugged. "The weather. The ridiculous roundabout intersections. The traffic on Dell Range. Anything, as long as she lets you inside."

Ana Maria looked suspiciously at Arn. "Why do I want to get inside her house?"

"Remember the wall with the shadow box hanging on it… that 'I Love Jenessa' wall with all the photographs?"

"That showed when Milt and Maddy adopted Jenessa?"

"That's the one. Grab a photo with your phone. I have the feeling we'll want to look at it later."

23

Haven Talish's campaign event at Little America began filling up an hour before the gubernatorial candidate was even scheduled to arrive and address the crowd. Arn was in that group who arrived early, though he waited out in the hallway, watching the room fill with adoring voters. The last thing he wanted was to sit towards the front where Haven could spot him. So, Arn bided his time until there was little more than standing room only and the crowd had spilled into the hallway before he joined others in the far back awaiting the canned speech Haven would give.

When he appeared from a side room and stepped up to a podium, cheers erupted from the crowd. Haven played the voters like a fiddle, letting them clap and cheer and yell "Talish for Governor" until, at last, he held up his hands, and the crowd gradually quieted. He thanked them while he pulled notes from his coat pocket and looked over the crowd with that pregnant pause he must have learned at Toastmasters. Arn leaned against the wall, tuning out the speech that Haven could have been reading off his campaign flyer. After what seemed to Arn like an hour, Haven wrapped up his spew with a plea to contribute to his run. "Give generously. For the sake of the state of Wyoming," he ended with, and the people began filing out of the room, many dropping campaign contributions into a plate at the exit like they were giving to a traveling evangelist.

Arn elbowed his way through the crowd toward Haven, talking and laughing with voters gathered around him, and it wasn't until Arn had reached the podium that Haven noticed Arn standing in front of him. His smile faded, and he bent and whispered, "I told you before to call my office if you want to talk about… things."

"I did, but that bulldog-of-a-receptionist gave me a date to see you three weeks from now."

"Then we will talk in three weeks—"

"Unless you want me to ask—in a loud and commanding voice—that I need you to talk about Gene Woods being shot. Yell that the police have interrogated you about it. Do you think those contributions will come in so readily then?"

"The police interrogator cleared me of any suspicion."

"Then, surely you won't mind talking with me as soon as these people clear out?"

Haven forced a smile and looked about to see if anyone had heard Arn. "Meet me in the entryway in ten minutes."

Arn grabbed a cup at the coffee shop before heading to the entryway. He stood looking at the four-foot stuffed penguin behind glass, the goofy thing looking like a judge about to hold court, as he waited for Haven to walk through the double doors.

"Now, isn't this better talking, you and me, without all the other… groupies hanging around?"

C. M. Wendelboe

"Let's get this over with, Anderson. What is it you want?"

"Tell me about Gene Woods's shooting last night?"

Haven shrugged. "I've already told Davis and Sgt. Ames."

"Humor me."

Haven took a deep, calming breath. "Gene invited me to the Albany for supper. He intended to throw the weight of his company behind my campaign. He was to have his accountant issue a draft to my campaign the next day. We left, and the next I knew, the cops were banging on my door. I even agreed to take a polygraph, but Detective Davis said that wouldn't be necessary."

"When the dinner conversation came to the night Josie Dexter was killed, what was said?"

"We never talked about that."

Arn guffawed. "Perhaps the most damning night for either of you—being suspects in a woman's murder—and you guys didn't discuss it?"

A slight tic at the corner of Haven's eye told Arn the man was lying. "I find that hard to believe, but I'll let it pass for now—"

"I really have another appointment—"

"Not so fast," Arn said. "Ana Maria tells me you were in the Denver area the days Happ St. John and Eddie Bragg were murdered." She had told Arn nothing of the sort, but he threw it out there to gauge Haven's reaction. Once more, that nervous tic showed Arn the state's next governor was concerned about that information getting out to the public. "I can prove my whereabouts while I was in Denver those days. Airtight alibis."

Arn chuckled. "Another football ticket?"

Haven sputtered... "I can give you the names of the people who can vouch for where I was."

"Close friends, no doubt," Arn said. "I would expect you to line up nothing less than an *airtight* alibi, with the effort you went through to convince people you were away from Denver when Josie Dexter was shot."

"I don't like your tone," Haven said.

"And I don't like getting jacked around." Arn stepped closer, and Haven stumbled back against the case. He looked behind him and the penguin looked back. "For starters, I believe you and Gene had a not-so-friendly supper while you talked about Josie Dexter's murder. Something more happened the night your friends brought Josie to your house, and you have been less than truthful from the first time I asked you about it."

"I don't have to stand here and put up with this—"

"And another thing: I believe your investment plan—the tontine—dominated much of the conversation with Gene last night."

Haven laughed nervously. "Why should that even come up?"

"Because you and Gene are the only survivors. Because you are strapped for money, and cashing in on the tontine would bail you out."

"That would require Gene to be dead."

"You know that's my point. Coincidentally, he was shot right after you two ate supper together. If that first responder hadn't been there when he was shot and plugged the leaks, your financial woes would be no more."

"You're accusing me of shooting Gene when I don't even own a gun."

Arn smiled. "This is Wyoming—everyone owns at least one gun. Maybe yours is a 9mm. Maybe a .38."

"I am the last person the police suspect, tontine or not."

"Is that inside information from your girlfriend?"

Haven's face flushed and he came away from the penguin case. "Jenessa told me you were following us the other night. But for the record, she's not my girlfriend. We just hang around now and again."

"Right before heading to a motel?"

Haven smiled as if reliving something pleasurable. "We're adults and can damn sure do what we please. Now, this little tête-à-tête is finished."

*   *   *

"'Fraid we might be at a dead end." Ana Maria laid out her notes from the afternoon. "It was a quick conversation with Maddy before she had to run back to the tailor shop."

"Was she suspicious as to why you wanted to photograph Jenessa's 'I Love Me' wall?"

Ana Maria took the cup of hot cider Danny handed her and sat back in her chair while she stared at the white wall. "She just thought I was a fan. You going to tell me why you want a copy of that photo?"

Arn leaned across the plywood and took the picture Ana Maria had printed out. He donned his reading glasses and turned the photograph so he could see. "Guess my memory isn't going quite yet. Look here." Arn turned the photo so that Ana Maria and Danny could see what he pointed to. "That shadow box. All pistols. Except, if you look closely, you can see that one is missing. By the outline in the dust, my guess is it's some small snub-nosed revolver."

Ana Maria sipped the cider and shook her head. "All that means is that there was a gun in that shadow box at one time."

"Did I mention my memory's still good? The day we were at Maddy's talking with her, that shadow box was full," Arn explained. "Now there's one gun missing. My guess is it's a .38."

"Still can't do much with that." Danny took the photo and looked at it for a moment before he laid it back on the plywood. "Even if there were a .38 in there on the day you and Ana Maria visited Maddy, that don't mean anything."

"It means," Arn said, "that either Maddy or Jenessa wants to make sure that gun is not found. In case there's a search warrant for it."

Danny picked up the Sharpie and approached the wall. "If I hear you correctly, you're thinking Jenessa might be Gene's shooter now?"

"What I'm saying," Arn explained, "is both Jenessa and Haven had good reason to see Gene dead. Haven, so he could cash-in on the investment scheme; Jenessa, because Gene was at that party the night Josie was murdered. And he might possibility be the other man who helped Happ stuff the body into the dumpster."

24

Arn stopped by the hospital the next morning, but Gene was still in an induced coma. His daughter from Miami was due to arrive any time, and a priest had been called in to administer last rites. The ER doctor could tell Arn nothing 'on the record,' but 'off the record,' it didn't look good for Gene.

As Arn was leaving the Intensive Care Unit, Sgt. Ames entered the room. He glared at Arn and said, "What the hell brings you up here? Snooping into police affairs again, would be my guess."

Arn breathed deeply, calming himself before answering. "Let's say I am a concerned citizen. I talked with Gene a few times and he was affable. Hated to see him shot. Any ideas—"

"I wouldn't tell you if I had any," Ames said.

"Even if I had information to... trade?"

"What information? If you're withholding something germane to the case, I'll have your nuts in a jar sitting on my desk."

"You'd have to prove it," Arn said. "Which I doubt you could. Now, you want to talk over a cappuccino or not?"

Ames hesitated before answering, "Against my better judgment... lead the way."

They stopped at the hospital coffee shop, and Arn bought both of them a cup before motioning down the hallway. "Be better if we sit away from prying ears," and Arn led Ames to the cafeteria.

Arn walked to a corner table, the only other people this time of day were cafeteria staff taking a break, sitting at the opposite end. "Do you have any leads on Gene Woods' shooting?" Arn asked after he'd sat.

"Whoa," Sgt. Ames said. "I thought we were going to trade information. First, what do you have?"

Arn had long thought this morning, as he was sitting alone quietly looking at the white wall, if he should tell anyone involved in the shooting investigation about Jenessa. He was certain there had been a gun in that shadow box—a small-framed revolver—the day he and Ana Maria talked with Maddy that was now missing from the box. If he were wrong about Jenessa, and false allegations reached the police chief, it could ruin her career. Was it worth taking the chance? "You are one of the few here in town who knows about Jenessa's dancing life in Denver," Arn began. "But do you know her background, how she came to be adopted by Maddy Wells?"

Ames nodded. "I've long had an... interest in Detective Wells, and so, yes, I did research into her background. I know her mother was murdered."

"But did you know Gene Woods was one of the last to see her mother alive at a party, and that he may have had something to do with her death?" Arn explained that Detective Heinz of the Denver Metro Cold Case Unit had been working on Josie's murder but had made little progress. "It would appear Gene was at that private party at Haven Talish's house along with Happ and Eddie Bragg. And we know how they wound up."

"That's your information?" Sgt. Ames said. "Eventually, I would have uncovered it, not that it would tell me who shot Gene Woods."

"Might," Arn said. "Her mom—*adopted* mom and aunt, Maddy—says that Jenessa has been obsessed with finding her real mother's killer all her life, to the point that she applied to the police department hoping for some insight that would help her find the killer."

"And?"

"And if it were you who lost your mother to a murderer, what would you do?"

"Hunt the bastard down and ventilate him," Ames answered immediately.

"And that," Arn says, "is what might have happened." He opened his messages and showed Ames the photo Ana Maria had snapped of the shadow box and sent from her phone. Arn explained about the gun that was missing from the shadowbox, a small caliber gun that might be a .38, a possible caliber in Gene's shooting. A gun that was in the box that first day Arn and Ana Maria stopped by to talk with Maddy.

"I'd be more inclined to believe she would use her issued Glock 9mm than some wheel gun."

"But doesn't the department keep ballistics on officers' guns on file in case there's an on-duty shooting?" Arn asked. "Or an off-duty shooting?"

Ames nodded. "So, we can figure out who shot the suspect, especially if multiple officers are involved."

"Jenessa would know that. She would know if her duty weapon were used in a shooting, there would be a ballistic record on file," Arn said. "If she's Gene's shooter, she would likely use something besides her issued weapon."

"Something like a small .38," Ames breathed, almost a whisper. He sipped his cappuccino and seemed to be mulling things over when Arn said, "Could you get a look at that shadow box and question her as to where the revolver is that was there not a week ago?"

"There's not enough for a search warrant," Ames said before a broad smile crossed his face. "But I could question her about it with the implied threat that her stripping down in Denver might be leaked to the chief. That's if you don't come hunting me up."

Arn waved at the air. "That kind of threat would be for a good cause."

"To satisfy my curiosity, why are you down on Jenessa? Gene Woods probably had a dozen people he feuded with—business-wise—who would have wanted him dead. Why zero in on Jenessa Wells?"

"Ana Maria," Arn said. "You weren't the investigating officer, but I'm sure you read the report of her being choked out in Good Time Charlie's parking lot."

"Sure. I read the report. Another dead end. No suspects. The witnesses saw nothing. Nada."

"Ana Maria has a strong sense of… intuition. She is certain her attacker didn't intend to kill her. Her attacker used what Ana Maria is certain was a Vascular Neck Restraint. Like you police are taught in your custody control classes."

Sgt. Ames sat back and tipped the last of his coffee up. "All right. I'll lean on Jenessa to get a look at that shadow box and ask her about the missing revolver. Even though it's against my better judgment."

"It's for a good cause," Arn said. "Besides, it's not like you're going to get a date with her anyhow."

* * *

Danny stood with his hands on his bony hips, staring at Arn. "Brush that dirt off *right there*. I don't care what you get in the entryway, but the rest of the house… I busted my butt all day vacuuming drywall dust, and I am in a nasty mood right now."

"Not any nastier mood than I am." Carefully, so as not to get it dusty, Arn hung his Stetson on the coat rack.

"I know you said you had to call a wrecker for your Olds, so I guess Ana Maria was right about you screwing up that shift linkage."

"The linkage wasn't the problem," Arn said. "It was the four flat tires I had when I got back to my car in the hospital parking lot."

"Crap! Sounds like your day *was* worse than mine. Maybe a cup of my Vietnamese coffee will help."

"Couldn't hurt," Arn said and followed Danny into the kitchen.

Danny grabbed the eggs and Carnation milk. He turned the burner on under the tea pot filled with water and began frothing the eggs and milk. "One flat tire, I could see," he said over his shoulder at Arn sitting at the kitchen table. "But four? I would wager someone slashed them."

"Even if you were not a genius, you could figure out someone flattened them. Ripped the sidewalls with a knife or something. I just put those tires on last month."

As Danny put the coffee grounds into the top of the drip maker before adding water, he asked, "What did the security tapes show?"

"Hospital security cameras were down for repair," Arn answered. "Have been for two weeks, so I got no help there, and the police could find no witnesses."

Ana Maria came home and walked straight to the kitchen. "OK, give me the lowdown on your vandalism. Heard your tires were slashed."

Arn explained to her what he had already told Danny. "Ames call you and tell you about it?"

"No," she answered, stripping off her sweater and draping it over a chair. "The police dispatch most of their calls via their car computers. I happen to know that frequency. I am sorry, as now you'll have to spend the money for tires and not on a replacement linkage."

She set her briefcase on the floor and walked to where Danny was making his Vietnamese concoction. She drew in a deep whiff when Danny said, "You don't have to ask. I'll whip one up for you soon's I finish with Arn's."

She sat and leaned her elbows on the table. "Sounds like your day went about as good as mine. DeAngelo sent me to the Ice and Events Center to cover that health fair. If one more person asks me if I'm either constipated or have diarrhea, I *am* going to explode."

"I hear," Danny said, "that one out of ten people suffer from one or the other. I wonder if that means the other nine enjoy their condition?"

"Got me there," she said. "All I know is it cut into my Josie Dexter research."

"Detective Heinz came up with more when you called him?" Arn asked.

"I asked him if there was anything… anything in Josie's past that Neal Barton found that would yield any clues. This is all he had that we didn't." Ana Maria took a manila folder out of her briefcase and slid it across the table.

Arn flipped pages. He didn't recall the follow-up investigation a junior detective did some years after Josie's death, and he checked the date: a few years after Arn retired from Metro. "Here's a poor newbie to Metro Robbery-Homicide clutching at straws." Arn read where the investigator had talked with Maddy and Milt's neighbors about who might have come around, perhaps making trouble for Josie. The neighbors stated Josie dropped Jenessa off at Milt and Maddy's place at least once a week, and explained that Milt played with Jenessa, taking her to a local park and to an ice cream store a block away when he wasn't working.

The report showed a rosy picture of aunt Maddy and Uncle Milt until his double-gainer from their fourth-floor apartment in Arvada. The uniformed officer responding to Milt's untimely accident called him a green-eyed monster, noting that Milt had impaled himself on a fence when he fell and stared at the officer with blood-shot green eyes.

Ana Maria took the report back and scanned it one last time before stuffing it back into the folder and her briefcase.

"No change with Gene, I take it?" she asked.

"If anything," Arn said, "his condition has worsened. The ICU doc couldn't tell me specifics—damned confidentiality—but it looks like the doctor and his intensive care crew are preparing for the worst. On the plus side, Sgt. Ames is going to look into that shadowbox in Maddy's hallway."

25

Arn waved off breakfast and settled for a quick cup of coffee. "Where are you off to in such a rush?" Ana Maria asked.

"That was my question," Danny said. He stood hunched over a waffle iron wearing what appeared to be a woman's nightshirt that hung on his anemic frame, which Arn was certain he had rescued from a dumpster somewhere. "I'd say you need to eat something, but by the looks of you, I figure you can stand skipping a meal now and again."

Arn ignored his comment and set his empty cup in the sink. "Sgt. Ames wants me to come into the police department. Seems he asked Jenessa about that missing revolver, and he wants me to hear it from him."

"Hand me the butter," Ana Maria asked Arn. "You will keep me in the loop, whatever he says? My nightly broadcasts are getting pretty thin substance-wise. If I don't come up with something that's interesting—and drags the public's interest along—I'm afraid DeAngelo's going to send me to another branding, and I'd hate that."

"And miss out on another fresh calf testicle?" Arn laughed. "I'll call you later."

On the way over to meet with Sgt. Ames, Arn ran numerous scenarios over in his mind as to what Ames's new information was when he brought Jenessa in for an interview. That she surrendered the gun missing from the shadowbox and that there were enough ballistics in the bullet dug out of Gene to match the revolver was Arn's hope.

What he didn't expect was an angry Sgt. Ames at his desk with the shadowbox on the floor. "Don't bother sitting," Ames said. "This won't take long." He grabbed the shadowbox and placed it atop his desk. "Look familiar?"

"'Course. It's Jenessa's."

"Actually," Ames said, "it belongs to Maddy Wells. She was gracious enough to let me take it for a day or so. Just to prove a point."

Arn saw where the small revolver had hung beside a slab-sided 1911 pistol, a Colt Single Action Army, and a Walther PPK. "What point? Did you recover the missing revolver?"

Ames nodded. "I have it in my desk. Put your damn reading glasses on and look closer at these guns."

Arn donned his glasses and bent to look closer at the shadowbox, at the guns that formed the collection of antique pistols. At the *faux* guns. Replicas one could buy over the internet.

Ames opened his desk drawer and came away with a small-framed revolver, looking like any other Smith and Wesson snub-nosed, and handed it to Arn. "If you notice, there is J-B Weld glue smeared on the backside."

Arn hefted the replica, noting the light plastic gun had a crack across the barrel that was held together by the glue. "I don't understand—"

"What's not to understand?" Ames said. "I brought Jenessa in and hinted that she'd better level with me about this or I would go to the police chief. Her first reaction was laughter, and then she drove me to her house. Maddy Wells met us there and was kind enough to give up the shadow box for a day. This," he tapped the frame of the box, "was Maddy's present to Jenessa when she graduated from the academy. Damn hard to shoot anyone with a replica gun."

Arn handed the replica snub-nosed gun back to Sgt. Ames. "Well, aren't I the dumbass—"

"More than that," Ames said. "You're a *horse's* ass for even getting me in involved in this... accusation. After we got back here, Jenessa blew up, it finally sinking in with her that I actually thought she might have shot Gene. 'I want those brutes who killed my mother behind bars,' she yelled, 'but I wouldn't murder them!' And with that, she stomped out of my office and right up to the Senior Detective's office. She said she needed to take a couple weeks off to get her head right."

"You didn't tell anyone—"

"That she's a stripper?" Ames said. "I did not. I figured I'd done her a big enough injustice, accusing her of being the one who shot Gene Woods."

What Arn feared had happened: his persistence based on probabilities that Jenessa had avenged her mother's killers had come to fruition—she had been falsely accused by Sgt. Ames. And although he had told no one about Jenessa dancing in

Denver, or his own suspicions about Gene Wood's shooting, the stigma of Ames's accusation would stay with her for a long time. "No wonder she took a couple weeks off."

"As for 'a couple weeks off'," Ames said, "make sure you and me don't run into one another for *at least* a couple weeks. It's going to take that long to get this stench off of me. Now, there's the door."

*   *   *

Ana Maria tucked her legs under her before covering herself with a blanket. "I wouldn't beat yourself up over it," she said to Arn. "Danny and I both thought there was enough circumstantial evidence to bring Jenessa in for questioning."

"You'd be as pissed as she was," Arn said.

"Not necessarily." Danny entered the TV room, balancing three pie plates topped with whipped cream. "It would all depend on how Sgt. Ames approached Jenessa."

"Danny's right," Ana Maria said as she dug the remote from the side pocket of her recliner. "From what I know of Ted Ames, he is no suave communicator. I can see him outright accusing her of attempted murder in Gene's shooting. Even someone as even-minded as me would bull-up with that."

That forced Arn to chuckle. *Ana Maria even-minded*? She'd be as likely as not to kick Ames's behind if he accused *her* of shooting Gene.

"It appears we are back to looking at the only suspect left— Haven Talish," Ana Maria said. She pointed the remote, but it did nothing, and she tossed it to Danny to fix like he always did.

"Haven is the only one who would benefit from Gene's death. And I would wager he had something more to do with Josie Dexter's murder than he's letting on. There's a reason he went to great lengths to fabricate that alibi with the football ticket."

"You're figuring him for Happ and Eddie Bragg's murder?" Arn asked.

"Can you think," Ana Maria said, "of anyone with more motive than Haven to see those men dead if they were all in on Josie's murder? And with Jenessa scratched from our suspect list, and Haven profiting from cashing in on the tontine investment scheme, he floats to the top."

Danny jabbed the air with pieces of the remote. "I'm just wondering—"

"That's why we call you Wonder Boy," Arn said with a grin.

Danny ignored him and half-turned in his seat to face Ana Maria. "What I was wondering is—if Eddie and Happ were strangled to death, why would Haven change his MO and shoot Gene? *Forensic Files.*"

Arn stopped mid-mouth and laid his fork on the plate. "Hate to admit it, but you're right. Why would Haven change his MO? Plus, why would he risk a gunshot in downtown when he could silently strangle Gene, and it might be hours before his body was discovered?"

"I don't believe you guys," Ana Maria said. "It's obvious why Haven would switch his method of murder."

"Fill us in," Danny said."

"Have you forgotten how Gene is built?" she said. "It would take a very powerful person to strangle him. Gene would not go quiet into that goodnight."

"Haven's no slouch himself," Danny said. "Guy at Gold's Gym says he works out every day. Benches one-eighty. Not bad for his age."

"Certainly strong enough to *try* to strangle Gene Woods," Arn added. "But then again, why would he take the chance of Gene getting the upper hand? Eddie and Happ were little guys, so Haven wouldn't be risking much there. But Gene would be another matter."

"So you are still looking at Haven as Gene's shooter?" Ana Maria asked.

"I don't know," Arn said. "I just don't know." He stood and headed out of the room. "Maybe looking at the white wall will clear my head and I can think this through."

Arn walked into the spare room with the dry wall dust, and the bucket of mud in the way, and the chair in front of the plywood across the sawhorses that he had to dust off with his bandana, and sat. Just staring. How had this case grown to such a convoluted mess? Even though the man was a narcissistic ass, Arn didn't want Haven Talish to be the prime suspect. It didn't bother Arn that Haven had the backing of most folks here in Cheyenne, and—with the governor's election in a few months— perhaps the whole state. But Haven did have the most to gain by Gene's death. He was in financial straits, especially with the campaign draining his resources.

"I know we figured Haven to be the most likely suspect, but things are bothering me." Ana Maria, her blanket wrapped around her shoulders, entered the room and sat beside Arn.

"What's bothering you?"

"Jenessa," she answered. "I know it appears as if she wants

a sugar daddy, but Haven is old enough to be her *real* daddy. There's gotta be more to their relationship than that."

Arn grinned. "Is that the psychology minor doing the thinking?"

Ana Maria shrugged. "Just thinking aloud. You know it could be that Haven is her father-figure, especially since she never knew her real father."

"But she did have her Uncle Milt Wells as a stand-in father before he jumped off that balcony in Aurora."

Ana Maria shuddered. "I still see those dead green eyes flaring up at the photographer from that photo the night he committed suicide."

"And that's what bothering *me*," Arn said, returning to staring at the white wall. "I read the responding officer's report on Milt's death. Maddy said when Milt got drunk, he got depressed and talked suicide. She said she never thought he'd do it, but that night, he took a running leap off their balcony."

So, what's the bother?" Ana Maria asked. "You never investigated a suicide by fatal fall before?"

"You know that I have. Back when you were reporting for the Denver affiliate, you covered four or five of *my* suicide cases."

"Then what's eating at you?"

"What's eating at Arn," Danny said as he entered the room with a bucket of warm popcorn, "is that Milt had little reason to commit suicide." He shrugged. "Not to steal your thunder again."

"How did you know what was bothering me?" Arn asked.

Danny popped kernels into his mouth. "I told you, I just know things. Besides, that bothered me, too. Reminds me of a *Forensic Files* episode."

Ana Maria groaned. "This I have to hear."

Danny passed the popcorn bucket to Arn and sat on a folding chair. "The episode was one where a lady overdosed, an apparent suicide. But there was nothing in her recent life to indicate anything other than that she had enjoyed life. Never talked suicide."

"So, what did they find out?" Arn asked, setting the popcorn on the piece of plywood.

"That it wasn't a suicide after all. Her oldest daughter spiked her mother's milk with some dope and she OD'd. And *voilà*, the daughter inherited her mother's estate. Until she was convicted of murder."

Ana Maria tossed popcorn in the air and caught it in her mouth. "The responding officer's final report said Maddy was constantly riding Milt over his gambling problem. They had gotten behind on some bills. The bank even threatened to repossess his car."

"Was he hopelessly in debt?"

"Not *hopelessly*, but in enough trouble where he might have thought suicide was the only way out."

"Wouldn't be the first time someone killed themselves over money," Arn said, "but with the suicides I've investigated involving money, the victims were *way* over their heads with no other way out. Was Milt in that bad a shape?"

Ana Maria shook her head. "The officer handling his accident checked Milt's background and didn't feel he was that far in debt that he would be hopeless." Ana Maria stood and wrapped the blanket tighter around her shoulders. "And so now we're back to what's bothering you."

"Milt Wells—by all accounts—adored his niece. He took her to parks and then arcades when she got older. He willingly took Jenessa in as his own daughter after Josie's murder. He and Jenessa were practically inseparable. That's what's bothering me... would Milt put someone he loves through such pain of losing him, just a few years after Jenessa had lost her mother? Would he kill himself knowing his niece would suffer?"

"I see your point," Ana Maria said. "But if Milt were a total A-hole he would. If he thought there was no other way out of his debts. Who knows the logic behind some of the suicides we've covered? Especially if someone is drinking like Milt was that night."

"She's right," Danny said. "*Forensic Files* often cannot determine the motive behind some suicides. Especially if they didn't leave a note."

"Which Milt did not," Ana Maria said.

She grabbed the bucket of popcorn and started for the door. "*Survivor* starts in ten minutes. Maybe that'll get our minds off this thing."

26

Sometime during the third pot of coffee, Arn set aside the police and medical examiner's reports he'd laid all across the plywood. He started to stand when he dropped back down into the chair, exhausted.

"Maybe if you go to bed, you'll think clearer in the morning." Ana Maria tied her terry cloth robe at the waist and sat beside Arn.

"Am I keeping you awake?"

"You're not keeping me awake," she replied. "But Danny banging around the kitchen... now that's making noise."

Arn rubbed his eyes and looked towards the door, expecting the thin Indian to come in with another pot of coffee. "Sorry, but he felt obligated to keep me fueled with this," Arn held up his coffee mug. "There's just something here I am missing, and I can't put my finger on it."

"With the police reports?"

Arn shrugged. "No, with the autopsy reports." He slid the folders with copies of the medical examiner's findings over to Ana Maria. "I got to thinking of that *Forensic Files* episode

Danny mentioned, and compared again Josie's murder with Happ and Eddie's. Strangled. All three, yet Gene was shot. A killer usually doesn't changer MOs—"

"Unless they learn and evolve."

"I just don't know," Arn said, shuffling through the autopsy reports when... his eyes fell once again on Milt Well's suicide, and he picked it up for the umpteenth time. "Autopsies back in the day like Milt's weren't so much done sloppily; it was more that the MEs were so overworked. Whenever a suicide victim landed on their table, they tended to not give them the thoroughness they deserved so they could move on to homicides and questionable deaths. They would often rely almost exclusively on the responding officer's observations."

"Can't say as I blame them." Ana Maria poured herself a cup of coffee and propped her leg on the sawhorse. "I can see the medical examiners being more than a little overworked in a place as big as Denver Metro area."

Arn shuffled through Milt Well's toxicology report and rubbed his eyes. He started slipping it into the pile of autopsies when he paused, picked up the report, and put his reading glasses back on. "What the..."

"What?"

"Milt Wells... look at his B.A."

Ana Maria set her cup down and put her own reading glasses on. "Blood alcohol was .02."

"Right," Arn said. "Milt wasn't drunk after all. That .02 reflects Milt may have had one beer in his system." Excitedly, Arn stood and started pacing. "So, there had to be some compelling reason Milt killed himself other than he got drunk and felt overwhelmed by his debts." He faced Ana Maria. "In your research, did you find out if Milt had any other life insurance policy?"

"Just that one small policy he and Maddy took out a year before Milt died," Ana Maria said. "But there was a suicide clause that stipulated the insurance company would not pay out with a suicide for the first two years. Pretty standard. Maddy couldn't collect on the policy, if that's what you're thinking."

"Then, once again, why the hell did Milt kill himself?"

"Guess you'll have to ask Maddy that. But in the grand scheme of things, does it really make any difference?"

"Probably not," Arn answered with a deep sigh. "But finding out the real reason he died by suicide might steer my investigator's mind to the real reason I'm stumped."

Ana Maria picked up the police reports, all the interviews and shoddy investigation into Josie Dexter's death along with Milt's apparent suicide. Added to that stack was the Metro Denver files on Eddie Bragg's and Happ's homicides, and there was enough to fill a banker's box. "You're right—the answer is somewhere in here."

"But what's the question?" Danny asked.

Ana Maria paused until she finally laid the report back onto the makeshift plywood table. "I don't know," she said, a wearied look on her face. "But, by God, I'm going to figure out what the question is before I leave this room."

"I understand what you're going through." He stood and rubbed his eyes. "I need to see Maddy and ask her my own questions."

"That might not be so easy," Ana Maria said. "Seems like the last time you talked with Maddy it was… a contentious conversation, if I recall your words. It'd be especially contentious now that Sgt. Ames all but accused Jenessa of murder. All because you felt the missing 'gun' in the shadow box might be the weapon that drilled Gene Woods."

"I gotta try." Arn set the carafe of coffee aside. "Gotta chance it. As soon as I get a few hours' sleep."

* * *

Arn parked a block away from Maddy's Place, certain that, if she saw him parked in front of her tailor shop, she would bolt to the back room, and he'd never get a chance to talk with her. He walked to within ten yards to look through the large window. She stood by a clothes rack as she showed a middle-aged lady a sequined vest. When their conversation finished and Maddy walked away, Arn waited until her back was turned before entering the business.

The same giggly receptionist Arn had dealt with before smiled at him until she recognized him, and the smile faded. She turned and walked quickly towards Maddy, but it was too late. Arn reached her first and said, "Do you have a moment?"

Maddy spun around and immediately glared at the receptionist as if she had failed in her duty to warn Maddy if Arn stopped in. "I thought I made it clear after you all but accused Jenessa of shooting Gene that I didn't want to talk with you."

Arn held up his hands as if in surrender. "Just a few questions and I'll be out of your hair. It's about Milt."

Maddy's eyes darted from two different customers lingering around the store before motioning Arn to a quiet corner of the shop. "It had better be only a few questions. I'm busy. Now, what do you want to know about Milt?"

"You said your husband got depressed and suicidal when he was drunk—"

"I told that to the responding officer in Denver the day Milt threw himself off that balcony. It's all in the officer's report."

"Except Milt wasn't drunk," Arn said, carefully watching for any tells that indicated Maddy was lying when she said, "That's nonsense. He was drinking that day."

There was no indication she was being untruthful. Either she really believed Milt was drunk that day, or Maddy was a practiced liar. "His toxicology report came back with a .00 B.A."

"I don't understand… perhaps he was under the influence of some drug. That'd be possible."

"Possible," Arn said. "Back then they tested for only a few illicit substances, unlike today when there're over a hundred tests on tox reports." Arn leaned his back against the wall. "Did Milt take any drugs that you knew of, even prescription drugs that he might have had a reaction to?"

"Just his booze," Maddy answered. "At the time, that whole thing about Milt's suicide devastated me. After Josie's murder, we took out a life insurance policy, but Milt killing himself nullified it, and Jenessa and I got nothing." She stepped closer, her glare almost even with Arn's. "But what has this got to do with you accusing Jenessa of shooting Gene and saying she was in Denver stripping the exact dates Happ and Eddie Bragg were murdered? You might as well have come straight out and accused her of killing those men, too."

"I don't know if it had *anything* to do with them," Arn said, feeling the wind whipped from his sails. "I was hoping you could help me understand why Milt jumped off that balcony."

"I already told you he was a drunk and a gambler and got us into terrible debt. I know he had words with a couple men over money he owed a few weeks before he died. For all I know, we were in dire financial straits back then because of what he borrowed to feed his gambling habit. Now, if there's nothing else, *one* of us has to work for a living." She turned her back on Arn and walked off; the interview, such as it was, over.

As Arn left Maddy's Place, he realized he didn't know what he had expected, coming here and opening new wounds with Maddy Wells. Whatever was stuck in the back of his mind, he could not jar it loose.

27

As Arn and Ana Maria walked toward Metro headquarters, they had to step around two homeless men sleeping on the sidewalk. "When I was with Denver PD," Arn said, "we would arrest these guys for vagrancy. Now, the police just ignore them."

"Not much else they can do," she said. "The new council and mayor are taking a more progressive stand."

"I would wager that legalizing marijuana doesn't help any," Arn said with a grin. "Though I bet you wouldn't know anything about that."

"Back in my college days, I did a dube now and again at parties. I told you that. We all did it. But the weed they're selling now is a lot more potent than what I dealt with when I was in school. Back then, sinsemilla was the strongest out there with a THC content upwards of seven-and-a-half percent. But what they grow nowadays... fifteen to twenty percent THC content is normal. Smoking stuff that strong has been known to trigger episodes of psychosis in some people similar to schizophrenia."

Arn's eyebrows raised. "You're worried about this?"

"Relax," she replied. "I'm not smoking anymore. I've just done some research into the problems in Denver that have been spilling over the border into Wyoming. I wanted DeAngelo to allow me airtime to present it to the public, but he's been sitting on the drug fence and wishes to remain neutral."

Ana Maria walked to the receptionist and asked for Detective Heinz. After a brief moment, they were rung through the door, and a lady waited in an ice-blue blazer emboldened with the Denver PD logo. "We know where Detective Heinz's office is by now," Ana Maria said.

The officer said with no emotion, "Maybe so, but we can't have people wandering through our building alone. Please stand by this wall."

Ana Maria and Arn stood while the officer ran a wand over them for potential weapons. "No gun?" she said to Arn. "Everyone from Wyoming carries a gun."

Arn had wisely left his snubbie in the car after he'd parked, knowing the security measures that the agency performs. "I'm pure as the driven snow."

The officer said, once again with no emotion in her voice, "Come this way."

When they arrived at Roger Heinz's basement office, the door was open, and he waved them in. Unlike the woman officer who escorted them, Detective Heinz grinned, stood, and walked around his desk to greet them. Like he was happy someone interrupted his day of pouring over cold case files.

"Any progress on Josie Dexter's murder?" Maria asked, coming right to the point of the visit.

Heinz's smile faded, and he walked back around to sit behind his desk. "Not on hers. But I did clear up the identity of a homeless man who was murdered twenty-one years ago."

"DNA?"

Heinz nodded. "That's some magic, huh? Identifying people after that long."

"Want to try working your magic on Josie's case?" Ana Maria said.

"How's that?"

Ana Maria sat in one of the hard metal chairs in front of Detective Heinz's desk and rested her elbows on it. "By finding out who was Jenessa's father."

"Milt Wells was, after he and Maddy adopted her."

"No, I mean her biological father."

Detective Heinz thumbed through the folders on his desk and withdrew one that he opened up. He pulled out a copy of Jenessa's birth certificate. "All it lists is Josie's name. The father's is blank."

He showed it to Ana Maria, though Arn knew she already knew Josie never named Jenessa's father. "Neal Barton didn't work much on the case but he did check into Jenessa's father. Why?"

"DNA," Ana Maria announced. "What if her biological father was one of Josie's clients. Or some prominent man who didn't want anyone to know he'd had a baby by a streetwalker."

"You're thinking blackmail?"

Ana Maria nodded. "Maybe Josie was hurting for money. It's not a stretch that—as she got older—her... *marketability* might wane. Perhaps she wanted insurance for her little girl. Might there be the possibility of DNA in your database that would match Josie's?"

Heinz sat back and began twirling a red lock of hair that had fallen around his ears. He badly needed a haircut. With his harrowed look and three-o'clock shadow, he reminded Arn of the code breakers he'd read about in the Second World War, stuck in one small office for days. Overworked. Just like Arn thought Heinz was. "I don't know that there would be any record of her father. There would need to be some forensic sample of Jenessa… Hair, blood, or saliva."

"I think I can get Jenessa to give me a swab of her mouth," Ana Maria said. "She allegedly wants to find her mother's killer as badly as we do. Finding her biological dad might go a long way to finding out who murdered Josie. If I approach Jenessa the right way."

"There would have to be a DNA match in our database, and that's not likely."

"Not so fast," Arn said. He popped a piece of gum and offered Heinz a stick to replace his pencil end. "About the time I started at Denver PD, the Detention Facility was collecting swabs from intakes. DNA was rather new then, but Denver was on the cutting edge."

Heinz chewed his gum and looked at the end of his pencil like he wanted to gnaw on that instead. "So, you think someone arrested back in the day might be Jenessa's dad?"

"Back in the day, or a newer arrest," Arn said.

"I don't know—"

"Think for a moment who Josie Dexter's clients were—the possibility they were less-than-stellar citizens is pretty good. One of them may have been arrested back then, or may have since been locked up. What do you have to lose?"

"I don't know. The state lab is inundated with DNA requests—"

"But just think about it, Roger," Ana Maria said, her voice softened. "It's the old cases getting solved by whiz-bang forensics that make headlines. That make *Forensic Files*. That might be your ticket out of this dungeon, working your tail off. Working fresh cases instead."

Detective Heinz dropped his pencil on the desk and looked about his tiny office with the dented gunmetal gray desk, the metal folding chairs, one shelf of a bookcase broken. "You really think Jenessa would give you a swab?"

Ana Maria nodded. "And I could run it back down to you as soon as I have it."

"Wouldn't be evidence I could ever use in court."

"But it would show who her biological dad was. If he is in your DNA database. There may be a reason Josie didn't name Jenessa's father."

A smile crossed Detective Heinz's face and he looked about the office once again. "The sooner, the better, so's I can sweet-talk the lab techs into expediting the sample and the search."

* * *

They passed on the goofy cliff divers at Casa Bonita this trip and pulled into a Wendy's just off Interstate 25. The crowd was light this early afternoon, and Arn was certain no one overheard them. "Somehow, I have the belief that you don't think Detective Heinz will have any luck with the DNA search of local criminals."

Ana Maria dipped a French fry into the tiny ketchup cup and waved it in the air to emphasize her point. "You are so astute.

I'm more expectant that there will be a DNA match between the four guys who were at Haven's house for that private party the night Josie was killed."

"Why do you think along those lines?"

Ana Maria stuck a straw into her soda cup and lowered her voice as if there were people close enough to hear. "By all accounts, Josie readily went to Haven's house with no coercion that night after the bachelor party."

"Just means she saw an opportunity to make some extra money."

Ana Maria leaned forward and said, "I'm not a mother, but I am a woman who has thought about being one ever since I was of age. I am certain, if I had a young daughter at home, that I would be discriminating as to just whose house I went to party at. Would I, if I had such a daughter, chance leaving her an orphan because I went to some psycho's house? Not on your life."

Arn finished off his chili, knowing he'd pay for it later, and washed it down with soda. "But Josie's profession in itself was perilous. You know how many sex workers wind up dead along the side of the road or in some ditch. Josie took chances every night she hit the street."

"But," Ana Maria said, "Josie was a cut or two above your everyday streetwalker or lot lizard prowling truck stops. Putting myself in her place, with a little girl at home, I would still be cautious where I plied my trade. The fact that Josie lived that lifestyle for as long as she did would suggest she'd be wary just from experience. And I think she was careful that night as well. I'm betting a DNA comparison will match one of the four guys."

"You might have a point there," Arn said. "At least one of the men who was involved in her death that night—Happ St. John—might be a match."

Detective Heinz reassured them earlier that there existed evidence in banker's boxes of every unsolved homicide, and there would be hair and blood samples taken at the time still in there. If Ana Maria could sweet-talk Jenessa into giving a swab, at least two of the men at Haven's house that night could be compared. And it would be an easy matter to obtain Gene and Haven's DNA samples for comparison.

"When are you going to approach Jenessa for that swab?"

Ana Maria patted the evidence swab with the protective vial in her pocket that Detective Heinz had given her. "As soon as we get back to Cheyenne. Maddy will be at her tailor shop. I called, and Flambé isn't stripping tonight, so I suspect Jenessa's at home. Then I'll run it back down to Heinz."

"I'd offer to go along," Arn said, "but somehow I got the feeling that she still doesn't like me."

"Maybe," Ana Maria said, "you ought to soften your approach to people."

Arn grinned. "That'd be as boring as hell."

28

Ana Maria walked into the makeshift war room with the white board marked up with possible suspects and scenarios and stood in front of Arn and Danny sitting at the piece of plywood they were using as a table. She slapped a piece of paper against her hand while she grinned like a Cheshire Cat. "You know what I wish I had right now?" She said excitedly before answering her own question. "I wish I had that big board right here and Vanna White to turn letters. Make you guess what's in my hot, little hands."

Danny tapped the side of his head. "She sound a little touched to you?"

"No other way to explain her running in here and hopping around like a wild person," Arn said before turning to Ana Maria. "What are you so excited about?"

She held the folded paper in front of her. "What I am talking about is *this*—it's the results of Colorado's lab making a positive match with that swab sample I got from Jenessa. Detective Heinz thought I'd like it sooner than later and had a courier deliver it a few moments ago to the TV station. And I would bet neither of you could turn around enough letters to spell the name of Jenessa's father if Vanna herself were in this very room turning them."

Arn sipped his cold coffee as he studied Ana Maria. He had never seen her this animated. "We haven't turned enough letters yet. We have no idea who the crime lab matched with Jenessa."

"For heaven's sake," Danny said, "will you let us in on the secret?"

Ana Maria wasn't ready to give up her hard-won piece of the puzzle just yet, as she turned to the white wall and said, "Whose name is *not* up on that wall?"

Arn stood and joined Ana Maria staring at the suspects' names scribbled there. "Everyone we've figured as a suspect is there in one column or another."

"Except," Ana Maria paused for a long moment before announcing, "Milt Wells. He was Jenessa's biological father."

Arn took the lab paper and confirmed that, indeed, Jenessa's DNA sample and Milt's were a match. "How'd they get Milt's DNA? His death was a suicide. They don't normally keep evidence on suicides."

"His arrest," she answered, "for a DUI in downtown Denver a year before his death."

"But Milt wasn't drunk," Danny said. "He was having diabetic issues, and the case was dismissed. You read it."

"But not before he was booked in at the detention center." Arn nodded. "Part of that booking process would have been submitting to a swab of his mouth."

Ana Maria took back the lab result. "And now I'm going to talk with Maddy. I think I'd like a witness."

"She'll raise hell if she sees me one more time," Arn said.

"So that this doesn't become public," Ana Maria said, "she would gladly suffer your presence while we talk in private."

*   *   *

The receptionist said Maddy had left for home for lunch, and Ana Maria and Arn sat on a bench down the street from Maddy's place. They had discussed it on the way over here and agreed they would let Maddy tell Jenessa who her father was. She was probably at home, and the last thing they wanted was for anyone besides Maddy to break the news to her.

"I wonder if Milt had to pay for sex like everyone else," Ana Maria said.

"How so?"

"Milt and Josie—she was his sister-in-law, and yet, he obviously had sex with her at some point. At least once, Milt must have cheated on Maddy, and I wonder if it cost him money, or if it was just a moment of indiscretion between them."

"We might soon find out," Arn said and nodded at Maddy walking the sidewalk toward her tailor shop. She was nearly to the bench when she saw them and stopped abruptly, her eyes darting about as if she were looking for an escape route.

Ana Maria stood and approached her.

"I've got nothing to say to either one of you! Can't you people just leave me alone? What the hell is it this time?"

"Milt," Ana Maria answered, then lowered her voice. "We thought you might want to discuss him being Jenessa's father here, away from prying ears."

"Whatever the hell are you talking about?"

"Did you know he was Jenessa's dad?"

Maddy's head slumped, and she imperceptively nodded. "I knew."

Without looking back, Ana Maria walked to the bench where Arn was still seated. Maddy followed and looked down at Arn. Sorrow filled her eyes—not the fierce animosity she'd showed the last two times he talked with her. She sat between him and Ana Maria and asked, "How did you find out?"

As Ana Maria told Arn previously, she explained how she'd suspected that one of the four men at Haven Talish's that last night might be Jenessa's father, and that he had followed Josie out of the house to silence her. But—like Arn and Danny—Milt was the last one she suspected. "Did Josie and Milt have an affair?"

Maddy looked down as she kneaded one callused hand with the other. "My sister came to me one afternoon, bawling her eyes out like a fool. She said she and Milt got drunk one afternoon while I was working. I confronted Milt. He said it was a one-time thing, and I believed him."

"Must have strained the relationship between Josie and you," Arn said.

"Our relationship was already strained," Maddy answered, "by Josie's lifestyle, which I did not approve of. But if you're wondering if Milt was the other person stuffing her body in that dumpster, he was not." She pulled up her sleeves and bared her arms. "And neither did I. I held no grudge against that one day of indiscretion. See, no eagle tattoo."

"That never crossed my mind," Ana Maria said, even though it had crossed Arn's. People could get rid of tattoos, but the process still left traces, and he saw none on Maddy's arm. He made a mental note to fully read Milt's suicide report to find out if the investigating officer saw such a tattoo on Milt's arm.

Maddy sat in silence, watching a trolley bus full of gawking tourists roll by to tour the Old West town. "It doesn't mean I didn't still love Josie."

"But it would account for Milt being so attentive to Jenessa as a child."

Maddy nodded. "I wanted to tell Jenessa who her father was... tell me you didn't already give her the terrible news."

"We did not," Ana Maria said. "We figured it'd be best coming from you."

"Thank you for that. I'm not sure how Josie will take it—she was awfully close to her uncle... Milt."

"What was your reaction when you found out Jenessa was Milt's daughter?" Arn asked.

Maddy looked at him. "How would anyone feel? Before we were even married, Milt came around the house. Flirting with my sister who was some years younger and a lot prettier than me. I always wondered if he just married me to get close to Josie, but as far as I knew, they had sex just that once." She shook her head. "But that was one time too many, and then Jenessa was born."

"The worst part was that the secret might get out somehow, sometime if we'd stayed in Denver. That was the real reason I wanted to move out of there, but Milt would have none of it." She chuckled softly. "I guess the best thing Milt ever did was to commit suicide that night, leaving me and Josie free to move away from any ugly gossip."

She stood and looked down at them. "Now that you know, what are you going to do with this pearl of information?"

Ana Maria looked at Arn, then at Maddy. "Nothing that I can use in my broadcast. And I don't see how any of the lab results will help us solve Josie's murder, let alone Happ's and Eddie Bragg's. It's buried, as far as we're concerned."

They watched Maddy walk the last half-block towards her tailor shop. "Think she's telling the truth?" Ana Maria asked.

Arn thought about that. While talking with Maddy, he watched closely for any tells that she was lying. "She was mostly honest."

"Mostly? What did you pick up on?"

"Josie," Arn said. "When she talked about Milt coming around and flirting with Josie—there was a tiny, almost imperceptible tic at the corner of one eye."

"So, you do think she was lying?" Ana Maria asked.

"What I believe is that Milt and Josie's relationship was a lot more serious than she let on."

29

Danny walked out of the house into the backyard and yelled, "Where are you?"

"Under the Olds," Arn answered. He climbed out holding a shop light and shined it towards Danny so that the old man's face looked like an overripe prune in the darkness.

"Don't you know it's late?" Danny said.

"I decided to bite the bullet and try to fix that linkage one last time so it won't jam when I shift." Arn had spent the last three days messing with the shift linkage on the old car, but then he had little else to do. Ana Maria had taken Danny to Denver three days ago with Jenessa's mouth swab to hand off to Detective Heinz, leaving Arn at home with little else but to look at his car. The old man had been working his magic on the spare room while Ana Maria was buried in paperwork at the TV station. "Finally got it. Maybe." Arn figured, with the investigations grinding to a halt, that working under the car might jar something loose that would help. He was wrong. He was no closer to repairing his Oldsmobile than he was solving any of the crimes. "Why? Some reason I'm stepping on your sensibilities here in the backyard?"

"It don't bother me none." Danny held out his hand and helped Arn stand. They weren't spry men anymore. "What bothers me is I made a decent supper and I have to eat alone."

"Where's Ana Maria?"

"She's been in and out, flitting around like a hundred-pound Italian acrobat, worrying over that DNA sample matching Milt to Jenessa. Calling Detective Heinz every few hours to see if he can connect that information to Josie's murder. She sat in the reading room earlier, but she's not saying much."

Arn had seen little of Ana Maria in person since they had talked with Maddy, and otherwise, on her nightly broadcast. Arn just figured she was busy drumming up material to put on-air so DeAngelo wouldn't send her to another branding.

Arn used a shop rag to brush dirt off himself before entering the kitchen by the back door. He bent over the sink and used a good-sized dab of Dawn to cut through the grease. "My guess is her next nightly broadcast would be a burner if she aired the results of those DNA tests."

"But she still won't?" Danny asked.

Arn dried his hands with a flour sack cloth. "She's going to stick by her promise to Maddy and not make it public."

Arn sat at the kitchen table and drew in a long whiff of Danny's lasagna after he put a serving on Arn's plate. As he broke off a chunk of garlic bread, Arn closed his eyes and savored the pasta sliding down his throat. "You've outdone yourself this time."

Danny draped his apron over his chair and sat. "I tried."

By the time Arn finished his lasagna, Danny had wolfed down two portions and was dishing up more. It amazed Arn that the thin old man sitting across from him ate like someone Arn's size and never gained an ounce.

After they had eaten, Danny covered the dish of pasta with aluminum foil and set it on the stove top. "Ana Maria will love that whenever she comes home. Torte for dessert?"

"Does a fat baby fart?" He stood and poured coffee into his cup. "Meet you in the TV room."

Arn walked into the room and turned the set on, scrolling through the menu, when Danny entered with a saucer of dessert for each. He pointed at the screen and said, "There. That's an episode with Nancy Grace I haven't seen. That one has her investigating the Scott Peterson case."

Arn accepted the dessert and put the true crime program on. He settled into his recliner as he listened to Danny explain the forensics Nancy Grace also explained that investigators had used in the Peterson case.

As the program came to a close, Arn checked his watch and said to Danny, "I'm getting a little worried about Ana Maria. Getting mighty late."

"Isn't the first time she's stayed out late collecting material for her broadcasts."

"I don't know… she usually checks in."

"Give her a call and ask when she's going to be home."

Arn dug into his pocket and checked the ringer. It was turned on with no incoming calls but showed a message, and he opened it. "Crap!"

"Crap what?" Danny asked.

"Ana Maria sent a message. Said she didn't have any cell service at Curt Gowdy Park but that she could text."

"What in the world is she doing going to the park at this time of night?"

Arn donned his glasses and studied the text. "Haven Talish," Arn breathed. "He sent her a text and said he'd tell her everything about Josie Dexter's murder if she would meet him in the park at the amphitheater. Away from any witnesses."

"Do you think," Danny said, "this has anything to do with the DNA match of Milt and Jenessa?"

Arn pulled on his boot and said as he hurried out of the room, "Haven might have gotten wind that such evidence of Jenessa's father now existed," he said over his shoulder. "If that's the case, there might be some connection we haven't put together yet. But she ought to know better than to meet Haven alone. Twenty-five miles from town. At night. With no one to help her."

"Especially with Haven still a suspect in Gene Woods' shooting."

Arn ran to his upstairs bedroom and grabbed his backpack before coming back down the steps. He stumbled in the dark backyard and climbed into his Oldsmobile a heartbeat before Danny jumped in. "Get out. I'm gonna have to drive like a maniac, and I don't want you endangered—"

"That's about enough," Danny said. "I'm going, and the longer you sit there flapping your gums, the longer it'll take to catch up with her."

Arn had no time to argue and buckled his seatbelt. He backed out of the yard, kicked up dried grass and dirt, and speed-shifted into first gear.

And promptly locked the linkage up.

He worked the floor shift around like it was a mixing stick going through dried-up paint, but it never broke free.

He slammed his fist against the steering wheel, and it vibrated with the force.

"You should have let Ana Maria fix it rather than you mess it up more."

"Don't you think I know that?" Arn said. "Now, what the hell are we going to do?"

Simultaneously, they looked at the pathetic Yugo sitting beside the fence.

"I'll grab the keys," Danny said and ran into the house while Arn walked to the tiny clown car. He lobbed his backpack into what Yugo called a back seat, wiggling around to squeeze behind the wheel, just as Danny arrived with the keys and a battery jumper box. "Figured the thing wouldn't start after sitting so long."

Arn was almost hoping the car wouldn't start, but it did when he hit the ignition switch.

Danny set the jumper box aside and squirmed inside.

By the time they'd driven the first three blocks, the Yugo was going all of forty miles an hour.

"Can't this thing go any faster?" Danny asked.

"I'm pedaling as fast as I can," Arn answered.

They dodged a pickup truck twice as tall as the car. The driver looked down and grinned. Arn ignored him as he pulled onto Happy Jack Road, flooring the accelerator, coaxing the car as fast as possible.

"Do you really think Haven would hurt her?" Danny asked. "I mean, he's a bit slimy, but… killing a prominent figure in the community?"

"Out as far as the park is, who knows?" Arn said. "This is the end of camping season, so there might be one or two diehards, but they would be across the road from the amphitheater. And certainly no one walking around the amphitheater at night. He could do the deed and be back sleeping with Jenessa as his perfect alibi. Like you said, we've never entirely crossed him off as Gene Woods' shooter. My guess is ol' Haven Talish wants to live in that governor's mansion so badly, he'll do most anything to move in there."

The miles wore on, and Arn knew it would take another twenty minutes to get to the Hynds Road turnoff just across from the state park. "In my backpack, there's my revolver and a couple flashlights."

Danny fished inside the backpack until he came out with the snubbie revolver and the flashlights. Arn stuck the .38 in his trouser pocket and one of the flashlights in his belt.

"There's usually a streetlight shining down on the amphitheater."

Arn handed Danny the other flashlight. "If Haven thought this through—which I believe he is smart enough to do—he will have shot out the overhead light. Keep that flashlight close."

By the time they'd pulled off Happy Jack onto Hynds Road, Arn felt he'd gone ten minutes with his wrestling namesake Arn Anderson and his brother Ole, riding in the cramped car that he doubted the Minnesota Wrecking Crew could even jam themselves into.

Arn turned the one working headlight off and slowly drove Hynds Road, shining his flashlight out the window to navigate. At the end of the road was the Hynds Lodge, rented for weddings and reunions and larger gatherings. There was no light inside the lodge, and Arn stopped beside the trail leading to the amphitheater. He paused for a moment, recalling the layout of the trail leading to the granite amphitheater where he'd attended a wedding two years ago. "Careful," he told Danny. "The trail drops off as it nears the amphitheater."

They picked their way along the trail, flicking their flashlights on and off for seconds as they walked, until they arrived at the place where the trail ended and amphitheater seating began, benches made from local slabs of rock. Arn put his hand up to stop Danny. Arn squatted, looking down into the amphitheater. Ana Maria leaned against the back rock wall. She looked about, expecting Haven Talish, the overheated streetlight illuminating her face as she warily scanned the area. *So, Haven hadn't been savvy enough to shoot the light out.*

When Arn saw no other movement besides Ana Maria, he stood and started down the trail towards her.

She jumped and clawed into her purse for the gun Arn knew she carried. Her gun hand came out with her snubbie revolver, her other hand shielding her eyes from the light.

"Don't shoot," Arn said. "It's just me and Danny."

She lowered her gun for a moment before putting it back in her purse. "Sorry, but I'm just a little nervous. Haven still hasn't showed himself."

"What exactly did his text say?" Arn asked.

Ana Maria pulled out her phone and scrolled down. She handed the phone to Arn. He squinted as he read where Haven intended to come clean about Josie Dexter's murder. And nothing more. "You've talked with him on the phone—is that his cell number?"

"Burner phone," Ana Maria answered, still looking uphill to where the stone seats appeared to be members of a jury looking down on them. "I figure Haven wouldn't be so dumb as to lure me here with a call from his own phone."

Arn shielded his own eyes as he scanned the area. "How long have you been waiting?"

She checked her watch. "More than thirty minutes. I'm guessing he's a no-show…"

A rock rolling down the trail stopped Ana Maria. She squinted up the hill while she grabbed her gun again a moment after Arn skinned his out of his pocket.

Haven Talish picked his way down towards the amphitheater and stopped when he saw their guns drawn. He threw up his hands like Butch and Sundance had gotten the drop on him. "Whoa! I'm not armed."

"Come closer," Arn said, and Haven walked onto the amphitheater. "Keep your hands up—"

"What the hell is this—"

"Hands up," Arn repeated. "My grip on this gun is a little shaky, and I would hate for it to accidentally go off."

Haven raised his arms and Arn methodically patted him down but found no weapons. He lowered his gun and said, "You can drop your hands."

"What is this," Haven said, nervous, looking between Arn and Ana Maria, "some kind of shakedown?"

"I would ask you the same thing," Ana Maria said. "You're the one who said you wanted to meet out here."

"What the hell are you babbling about?" he asked.

Once again Ana Maria took her phone from her purse and

found Haven's text. She showed it to him. "Recognize this?"

"I don't understand. I never sent this, and this is not my cell number."

"Burner phone," she said. "Pretty smart."

Haven grabbed a bandana from his back pocket and wiped sweat from his forehead despite the night air being cool. "Look, you're the one who texted me wanting to meet out here."

"The hell I did," she said.

Haven cautiously reached into his pocket, and Arn quickly brought up his gun to point at the man's chest. "Easy, big 'un. Just getting my phone."

He slowly withdrew his cell phone from his trouser pocket and scrolled to his own texts to find the one he wanted to show Arn and Ana Maria.

The text read that Ana Maria had damaging information about Josie Dexter's murder that would impact his run for governor and asked Haven to meet her here. Arn saw that the cell number was not Ana Maria's. Probably another burner phone.

"I didn't—"

Arn cut Ana Maria short. The fact that Haven even responded to the text—though Ana Maria hadn't sent it—showed Arn that he knew more about Josie's murder than he'd let on. Knew things he wanted to keep secret. "I always got the feeling you were hiding something," Arn said. "Now with Ana Maria's new information she just got from the hospital—"

"Alright," Haven said and turned to Ana Maria. "Did Gene come out of his coma and spill his guts?"

Ana Maria picked up on Arn's ruse and remained silent.

"Your non-answer tells me he did." He wiped brow sweat again and blurted out, "For starters, I had nothing to do with Eddie Bragg's or Happ's murders. And I surely didn't shoot Gene. He's the only witness left to clear me of anything related to Josie's death."

"Do you need a witness?" Ana Maria asked.

When Haven hesitated, Arn knew he wanted to get events of that night off his chest that he'd held onto for thirty years. Arn laid a hand on Haven's shoulder and said, "Just tell us your version of events, and we'll see how they match up with Gene's memory of that night."

Haven leaned against the wall. He breathed deeply and began. "When Gene, Happ, and Eddie got me out of bed that night of the bachelor party, they wanted a... secure place to have sex with Josie. Pure and simple. No real partying to it."

"So, they woke you up," Arn said, "and you, what... had sex with her as well?"

Haven nodded and kicked a stone with the toe of his shoe. "I didn't intend to until I saw her. Damn, she was a looker. When Eddie called wanting to use my place, I had no intention of having sex with Josie. But the moment I saw her... she was the most alluring woman I'd ever seen, even if she was getting a bit old for turning tricks. I insisted that I be the first that night."

"I saw old photos of her before she was killed," Arn said. "A very beautiful woman. What do you say happened afterward?"

"What did Gene say?"

"Only that your version and his would be spot-on," Ana Maria lied.

"Alright. After I was... done with Josie and paid her the money,

I came out of the bedroom and poured myself a scotch while Gene went next. Then Eddie and Happ. As Gene told you, me and him and Eddie were sitting in my living room enjoying a drink when we heard a loud commotion coming from the bedroom. We rushed in just as Happ was climbing off Josie. She had his belt wrapped around her neck. She was obviously dead. We knew Happ was into the kinky shit, but never figured he'd take it that far. 'I didn't mean it to go this far,' he said, 'but she begged for it. I swear. Now, what am I going to do?'"

"So, she didn't leave your house with Happ and Eddie?" Ana Maria asked. "You carried her?"

Haven dropped his head. "Oh, God... do you know how badly I've wanted to set things straight through the years? We carried her out, the three of us. We put her in the back of Eddie's truck, and then we all drove around until we found a dumpster that had a lot of trash in it. Oh, God, I should have just gone to the cops then."

"Is that why you've been seeing Jenessa, to keep up on her end of investigating her mother's death?"

"That and more," Haven said. "Jenessa is a striking match for her mother—just as beautiful and alluring when she's not dressed in cop-frumpy. But as much as I enjoy Jenessa's company, I am ashamed to admit my self-preservation rose above my desire for her. Thought if I kept her close, she would keep me posted on any progress she made in her mother's murder."

"No offense," Ana Maria said, "but you are a tad bit old for her. How did you ever get close to her?"

Haven forced a laugh. "As plain as she always dresses, she didn't have many guys hitting on her. But I knew just how beautiful she really is, and I followed her to Good Time Charlie's one night. Struck up a conversation. When I told her who I was and that I expected to occupy the governor's mansion after the next election, she became a changed woman. Suddenly, she wanted a man in the worst way."

"You mean she wanted a sugar daddy," Danny said.

"And who are you?" Haven asked.

Danny puffed out his chest. "One of the private citizens—along with Arn and Ana Maria—looking into Josie's death. I have seen about every episode of *Forensic Files*, and believe me, some of the techniques I've seen on the screen we have used in this investigation to good effect."

"To Danny's assessment," Arn said, "you were a sugar daddy to Jenessa?"

Haven nodded. "She didn't need my money, working full-time as a cop and stripping, but she said she wanted to be a kept woman. She knew that as soon as I became governor, I would need a first lady. Then she could quit policing."

"How much did she know about you four guys that night?"

"I told her nothing, yet she might have found out about Happ stuffing Josie's body into the dumpster with Gene's help."

"So, the other man was Gene with Happ that night?"

Haven nodded. "Jenessa and I talked about your suspicions of her. By her own admission, she was in Denver when Happ and Eddie were killed. After a time, I got to thinking she might actually be their killer. And I suspect she's the one who shot and wounded Gene."

"Then you accuse my daughter of something else she did not do," a voice echoed off the amphitheater. Maddy slowly made her way down the steps, rifle in hand, pointed at them. "I know you pack," she motioned to Arn. "You drop that gun, and you, too, missy. I saw you stick one back in your purse. Haven?"

Haven's hands raised high. "Don't carry a gun. Never liked them."

"Then you're surely not going to like this one. Now, you four sit on the floor, and we'll all have a little chat."

30

Arn helped Ana Maria sit, and they all looked up at Maddy. "That was an interesting conversation you were having. Nice thing about this amphitheater is that the acoustics are great, even from up top."

"I would wager," Arn said, "that you bought a couple of burner phones to set up this little meeting."

"So astute," Maddy said, lowering her gun a few inches but holding it at the ready if she needed it again.

As Arn looked at Maddy with bags under her eyes, her lips that she kept wetting with her tongue, her eyes darting among all four, he knew she'd stayed up long hours setting this up, probably agonizing how to get rid of them. If he could just get her off her game. Distract her... "Sergeant Ames called and said Gene Woods named Jenessa as his shooter."

"Damn, you are an accomplished liar. You sound so convincing, even though I know that Gene died five hours ago and never came out of his coma. Good thing, too, as he'd name *me* as his shooter, not Jenessa."

"Then I am betting that Jenessa didn't kill Happ and Eddie

either," Arn said, stretching his legs, ready to leap erect if got the chance. That's if a sixty-year-old man could ever leap. "You did."

"OK, let's hear it," Maddy said, "and don't give me that cock-and-bull story that you told to the investigators."

"I won't do that," Arn said. Stretching. "But I will tell you that Detective Heinz is a sharp investigator. So is Sal Bass. Between the two of them, they will eventually figure things out."

"Just what do you think they'll figure out?" Maddy asked.

Maddy was fishing, Arn knew. That she intended killing them all here, now, he had no doubt. But she would not do so until she learned what evidence the investigators had that could tie her to the murders. "I speculated that you were strong enough to strangle Eddie and Happ—both small men, while you are… stout, shall we say. That time at your house when I saw you sewing leather with no palm protection, I knew you were strong."

Maddy flexed one hand. "As long as I've been doing it, I have developed a killer grip." She chuckled. "Literally."

"Before you dispose of us," Ana Maria said, "tell us, why didn't you kill Happ and Eddie years ago?"

Maddy shrugged. "I long suspected Haven there and his three amigos had killed Josie, but with no movement on the investigation these many years, I'd moved on. I had little more than a suspicion.

"Until Metro Cold Case Unit reopened the investigation and aired it on Denver television. That got me thinking about my sister once again. Conjuring up old frustrations. And hatred. I thought Jenessa's interest had waned as well, but reopening Josie's case gave her new incentive to find her mother's killer, too. When Jenessa ran down to Denver and obtained the police files—and those on the police database—I saw that at least two of them murdered Josie."

"I didn't kill her!" Haven blurted out.

"But you *did* have as much knowledge of her death as the others. You just admitted it to Arn and Ana Maria that all four of you drove Josie's body around until you could find a dumpster to stuff her in."

As Arn stretched his legs more, he looked about for something to use as a weapon when he spotted a rock the size of a baseball resting on the floor of the amphitheater. If he could keep her talking, perhaps Maddy would become even more exhausted, her reflexes slowed enough that Arn could snatch the rock. Distract her. In high school, he'd been an adept baseball player with a strong arm. Would that arm be as accurate as in his youth? Arn knew it wouldn't, but then, all he needed was to distract her long enough to rush her. Maddy might get off a shot. Perhaps two or three, but Arn was convinced one of them would live to tell her tale. He would take the chance and said, "Happ and Eddie weren't the first men you killed."

"This I gotta hear," Maddy said.

"Your husband, Milt." Arn scooted a little closer to the rock when Maddy snapped the rifle to her shoulder.

"Just stretching a cramp," Arn said, and Maddy eased the gun down. "Milt and Josie did the wild thing more than just that once, didn't they?"

Maddy nodded and a sad look came over her face. "I wasn't lying that day on the bench by my place when I told you I suspected the reason Milt came around our folks' house was Josie. I more than suspected—I knew. So, when he asked me to marry him, I was a little more than surprised. Why the hell would Milt want to marry a plain Jane when he could wait a few years until Josie was of age and marry her? But I didn't have anyone else beating down my door back then to marry me, so I jumped at the chance."

"You're saying he flirted with Josie even though she was underage?" Ana Maria asked.

Maddy nodded once again. "It started when she was about fourteen years old, and I know he continued teasing her as she got older. After we were married, my mother would bring Josie around the house for sleepovers when my mother needed to go out of town on business. Before she had that car accident and Josie had to move in with us. But that was all Milt did at that time that I know of, just teasing her. Josie would sit close to Milt. A little too close, but I blew it off..."

"When Josie got older," Arn asked, "did Milt's interest in her wane?"

Maddy seemed to mull that over for a long moment. "It did, and I always thought that was strange, because he'd been so touchy-feely with her when she was younger."

"But Jenessa's DNA is a match to Milt's." Ana Maria said. "At some point, he must have rekindled his desire for Josie, and they made love at least once."

Maddy chuckled. "Wasn't an ounce of *love* in that girl. Josie would not have laid down for any man—including Milt—without getting paid."

"Is that why you killed Milt?" Arn asked. "When you found out he was Jenessa's father?"

That nervous tic at the corner of her eye again. "I suspected.

The first time I *knew* he was Jenessa's father was the day you gave me the news. I had begged Josie many times to tell me who the father was, but she claimed she didn't know."

"As many men as she had," Ana Maria said, "perhaps she *didn't* know."

"The one thing I gave Josie credit for," Maddy said, "was that she always used a prophylactic. Isn't that true, Mister almost-Governor?"

Haven trembled with his back was against the rock theater. "She used protection that night. With all four of us. She insisted we wear one no matter how much money we offered her."

"Then the only thing I can think of is that Josie knew Milt well enough to know he didn't mess around," Maddy said, the gun drooping a few more inches. "Knew there was no danger of her getting an STD from him. If she was on the pill, it might have been one of the rare times it failed. But my guess is that it never crossed her mind that she'd become pregnant with him. So, what is your best guess as to why I killed my own husband?"

"Jenessa," Arn said immediately, inching closer to the rock as he feigned stretching his legs while he sat. Could he gather his legs under him quick enough to reach the rock and lob it at Maddy and hope the others would seize the moment and rush her as well? "Milt paid particular attention to Jenessa when she was only, what, seven or eight? Taking her places whenever Josie was… working. Milt would go over to Josie's apartment and then bring Jenessa over to your house, right?"

"He did."

"And when did his interest in Jenessa begin?"

"About a year before that when Jenessa was only eight. Why do you ask that?"

"Pedophiles tend to like a particular age range," Arn began. "And Milt did as well, by the sounds of it. He would have continued to do inappropriate things with her until she was little more than nine if he would have lived. Pedophiles have an age range they prefer. After the victim passes that particular age range, the pedofile will typically pass the child off to another pedophile they know who likes the age of victim."

"You found out about it, didn't you?" Ana Maria asked Maddy. "And you shoved Milt over the balcony. Sober. That's where you messed up—claiming he was drunk at the time he took the dive."

"I was so enraged when I realized Milt was molesting Jenessa, I just went berserk. Sure, I pushed him over the balcony. Shame it was ruled a suicide—I received no life insurance. But it was worth it to get rid of the bastard and to protect Jenessa."

"If there were ever extenuating circumstances," Ana Maria said, "that would be it. There's no doubt you would receive a light sentence in court."

"And as governor," Haven said, "I would consider a pardon for Gene's death."

Maddy laughed. "Do you really think you'll be elected governor if I let you all walk out of here? This news shark will plaster all of this all over the airwaves, and you won't be able to get elected dog catcher."

Arn slowly stretched his leg as he scooted another couple inches, now within grabbing range of the rock. His eyes met

Ana Maria's and Danny's, and Arn's darted to the rock, then back to them. They understood what he intended to do.

"Did you talk with Gene before you shot him?" Arn asked. If he could keep Maddy talking, he just might be able to snatch the rock. "Did he admit to helping dump Josie's body in the dumpster?"

"He rushed me that night in the parking lot," Maddy explained. "There was no time."

"But when the paramedics arrived," Ana Maria said, "his shirt was stripped off."

"I thought for sure he had an eagle tat on his upper arm, but he didn't."

Arn's eyes went to the rock then to Danny, who nodded imperceptibly.

Danny suddenly turned to Haven and screamed, "That leaves you, you son-of-a-bitch! *You* helped dispose of Josie's body and said nothing. *You* put us in this mess to get murdered."

Things kicked into slow motion for Arn, then Danny.

Danny leapt on Haven and his hands went for his throat just as Ana Maria threw her purse to one side, momentarily fixating Maddy's attention away from Arn.

Arn's hand fell on the rock.

He sat up and cocked his arm, sending the rock crashing into Maddy, hitting her arm holding the rifle as the rifle discharged.

Arn stood and rushed her, grabbing the rifle. Though she was fifty pounds lighter than him, Arn was impressed by Maddy's grip as another shot pierced the cool night air.

Arn squinted, looking up toward the stone benches.

Jenessa stood with her sidearm pointed in his direction. "I don't think you want to do that," she said. "Leave my mom be and step away from her."

31

Danny let Haven go at the same time Arn stepped back from Maddy. Ana Maria, trembling and frightened, moved to stand beside Arn. He didn't blame her. He was frightened as well, even before Jenessa arrived holding them at gunpoint.

Maddy clutched her rifle in one hand while she rubbed at the gash on her arm where the rock hit her.

Jenessa kept her pistol pointed at them as she walked the last few feet and stood beside Maddy. Jenessa looked at Maddy's arm and asked, "Are you alright or will you need to go to the Emergency Room when we're done here?"

Maddy said, almost with a snarl, "I'm not so wimpy as to need medical attention for this. Arn Anderson, I am going to enjoy this." She looked at Jenessa. "How did you find us?"

"I noticed a couple of burner phones you bought at Walmart sitting on the counter a couple days ago. Later in the evening, I saw that you had tossed them in the trash, and I got curious and looked at them. I saw that the only thing you used them for was to text Ana Maria and Haven to meet them here tonight. You should have smashed them to bits afterwards."

Maddy chuckled. "I guess, after tonight, it won't matter."

"Before you send us to the Great Beyond," Arn said to Maddy, "the least you can do is satisfy the curiosity of an old homicide detective."

She grinned wide. "Sure, what do you want to know, dead man walking? Or I should say, standing?"

"Why didn't you kill Haven before?" Arn asked. "At the same time you shot Gene Woods? You had already killed Eddie and Happ. The only one left was Haven."

"I had plans for Haven to kill himself in a couple days over his remorse of shooting Gene."

"I don't think I could ever have the... courage to kill myself," Haven said.

"I concur," Arn said to Haven, then turned to Maddy. "You were going to stage Haven's death as a suicide?"

Maddy nodded. "Complete with a suicide note. But I needed Ana Maria gone as well. She was on the verge of blaming Jenessa—on air—of killing Happ and Eddie Bragg just because she happened to be stripping in Denver on the same nights that I killed those two."

"But I had no such proof." Ana Marie's voice wavered. "It was just speculation."

"I couldn't take the chance," Maddy answered.

Keep the two talking, Arn said to himself, but there was no rock to divert both Maddy and Jenessa. Arn had one Hail Mary up his sleeve. The only thing he could think of was to rush them both and hope Ana Maria or Danny could get their hands on one of the guns. Arn wouldn't be able to grab one. By the time he ran to the pair, he would probably be shot multiple times. He had never thought himself a hero, but—if Ana Maria or Danny or Haven lived after tonight—maybe that's what they would lament at his eulogy.

"What do you remember about your uncle—father—Milt molesting you?" Arn asked.

Jenessa shook her head. "Honestly, I don't remember anything about it. That's a period in my life where I have a total blank."

"I took her to therapy," Maddy said, "when she started having nightmares. She's telling the truth—the therapist could never bring those years back for her. Which, in a way, is a good thing. Recalling being molested by a man you called *uncle* would be disturbing enough."

"Were you planning on murdering your mother's killers if you found them," Arn asked, relaxing his muscles, knowing relaxed muscles spring quicker. "Did Maddy just beat you to it?"

"What the hell do you take me for?" Jenessa said. "I am a law enforcement officer. I dig for the truth. No matter how painful evidence is—and it would have been painful just letting Happ and Eddie live—I would have gone to the prosecutor with what I found."

"So, all you wanted from me," Haven said, "was to pry information from me, and you weren't really interested in going to the governor's mansion?"

Jenessa laughed. "Me *really* interested in you? Believe me, the way I look when I dress to the nines, I know I can have any man I want."

"But I didn't tell you anything about that night."

Jenessa smiled. "I was working on that. You would have, eventually."

"And that's another thing I couldn't take a chance on." Maddy rubbed her arm and the bruise quickly forming. "When Janessa told me she was sleeping with Haven Talish—to see what pillow talk she could extract about her *mother's* murder—I knew I couldn't let her find out about the other man with Happ having an eagle tat on his arm after she told me she'd learned he had one."

"So," Arn said, "you were the other man who helped Happ stuff Josie's body in the dumpster that night."

Haven nodded and rubbed his arm as if rubbing the tattoo off under his shirt sleeve. "Gene and Eddie were too shook up to help. They were like blubbering fools, figuring we'd be implicated in Josie's death. But we knew we had to get rid of the body someplace."

"Enough!" Maddy said, waving her rifle in their direction. "All of you, move together."

"What are you going to do, Mom?"

Maddy looked sideways at Jenessa. "What do you think I'm going to do—I'm getting rid of the only witness who can connect me to the men who murdered your *real* mother."

Jenessa slipped her pistol into a shoulder holster and faced Maddy. "You can't kill these people."

"Of course, I can. And I need to."

"But all they did was uncover the truth," Jenessa said as she stepped around, putting herself between Maddy and the others cowering together at the back of the amphitheater.

Jenessa's move took Arn by surprise, and by the time he realized Maddy's gun was not on them, she had stepped around Jenessa and aimed her rifle at them once again.

And once again, Jenessa moved and blocked Maddy's aim. "Mom," she said as she gently put her hand on Maddy's rifle and lowered it. "You can't—"

Maddy jerked the gun away, but Jenessa remained blocking Maddy's aim.

Arn, poised, ready to rush her, paused, recognizing in Jenessa a true lawman. If there was a chance they could walk away from this night, he would give Jenessa a last chance to divert Maddy's attention.

"Mom, look at me."

Maddy did as Jenessa asked but quickly turned back to the four waiting for the inevitable.

"Mom, you didn't raise me to be a part of this. You raised me to be a decent woman, and you are the reason I was able to get into law enforcement."

"This has nothing to do with you."

"No? No matter what you do to these folks... no matter where you dump their bodies, they will eventually be found. And we—both of us—will be implicated."

The rifle's muzzle drooped slightly. "But they know what I did."

"And Ana Maria was right a few moments ago... any judge overseeing this case will see the extenuating circumstances. He or she will understand your desire to avenge the murder of your only sister. You will still serve time, but at least, you will eventually be paroled. I promise I will go to every parole hearing you have and plead your case."

"But I need to—"

"You don't want your gun going off with me in front of it."

Maddy's rifle dropped and she held it beside her leg as Jenessa eased it away from her.

Jenessa said over her shoulder, "Say nothing, or I might change my mind. Go. Mom and I will go into town and call the County Attorney as soon as we talk, just her and me. Now, *go.*"

Epilogue

Ana Maria walked into the kitchen, her nightly broadcast wrapped up for the night. She sniffed the air and asked Danny, "Is that meatloaf you're cooking?"

"You are so sharp. I used buffalo I bought at the Terry Bison Ranch last week. As a celebration."

"Celebration? For what?"

"For all three of us—and Haven Talish—walking away from an execution at Maddy's hand last month."

Ana Maria dropped into a chair and grabbed a Ritz cracker from a bowl in the center of the table. She closed her eyes as she nibbled on it before saying, "Odd how things as simple as the taste of crackers are so much more appreciated after a person has stared down a rifle and at certain death."

"You sound like you didn't have faith in me to come up with something to save us," Arn said, grabbing a few crackers before sitting back. "You know I always have some plan in mind."

"Rushing in and taking a few bullets wasn't much of a plan."

A month ago, after Jenessa rescued them and they walked out of the amphitheater alive, their discussions had regularly turned to how close they had come to being murdered. Arn had shared with them his plan to take some shots, hoping Ana Maria or Danny could leap in and disarm Maddy. "Your reporting has been remarkably empathetic towards Maddy," he said.

"Judge Hanes was as well," Ana Maria said. "At Maddy's initial appearance, he said he understood why she killed Gene Woods and wanted to ultimately murder Haven Talish. He alluded to dismissing the charge of first-degree manslaughter to a lesser offense but said he needed time to study the reports of Josie's death in Denver."

"Maddy's real trouble will come from Colorado prosecutors," Arn said.

"What did Detective Heinz say when you talked with him?" Danny asked Arn.

"The Chief of Detectives at the PD here drove down to Denver and gave him the lowdown on Maddy's arrest. Heinz got a lot of credit from the Metro administration, and they offered him a position in Robbery-Homicide working fresh cases."

"And Sal Bass?"

Arn chuckled. "Seems like The Ass is in the doghouse for not working with Roger Heinz in Cold Case."

Danny slipped on a pair of insulated mittens and opened the oven door. "You never did say what the police chief did after it came out that Jenessa was a stripper down in Denver."

"Arn saved her career," Ana Maria said as she draped a napkin over her knee and winked at him. "I'm surprised she didn't come over and give you a lap dance for going to bat for her."

"I think I'd have the big MI if Jenessa did that. But when I heard the chief had suspended her, pending an investigation, I paid him a visit. Laid out just how Jenessa saved us from certain death. I pointed out how much fortitude and character it took to turn in the only mother she ever knew. When I mentioned how the public would not want such an honorable officer fired, he agreed to lift her suspension."

Danny sliced each a piece of buffalo loaf and set their plates in front of them. When Danny began wolfing down his food, Arn said, "That's not like you. You usually take your time eating. It's almost painful to watch the way you draw out your meal. What's your hurry? You have someplace you need to be?"

"We all do."

"How's that?"

"Danny made a call," Ana Maria said, "to Sammy's Club. *Flambé* is headlining tonight, and Danny's springing for the cover charge for us."

Arn started to object before stopping himself. After what Jenessa just went through with her adopted mother, he thought, and after she'd saved their lives, the least they could do was attend one of her performances.

On second thought, Arn reasoned, he was rather looking forward to seeing her act once again and started wolfing down his own meat loaf.

About the Author

C. M. Wendelboe entered the law enforcement profession when he was discharged from the Marines as the Vietnam War was winding down.

In the 1970s, he worked in South Dakota. He later moved to Gillette, Wyoming, and found his niche, where he remained a sheriff's deputy for over twenty-five years. In addition, he was a longtime firearms instructor at the local college and within the community.

During his thirty-eight-year career in law enforcement, he served successful stints as police chief, policy adviser, and other supervisory roles for several agencies. Yet, he has always been most proud of "working the street" in the Wild West. He was a patrol supervisor when he retired to pursue his true vocation as a fiction writer.

Wendelboe is a prolific author of murder mysteries with a Western flair and traditional Westerns. He writes the Spirit Road Mysteries, the Bitter Wind Mystery series, as well as the Nelson Lane Frontier Mysteries, and the Tucker Ashley Western series. Wendelboe now lives and writes in Cheyenne, Wyoming.

If you enjoyed this book,
please consider writing a review
and sharing it with other readers.

Many of our authors are happy to participate in
Book Club and Reader Group discussions.
For more information, contact us at info@encirclepub.com.

Thank you,
Encircle Publications

For news about more exciting new fiction, join us at:

Facebook: www.facebook.com/encirclepub

Instagram: www.instagram.com/encirclepublications

Sign up for the Encircle Publications newsletter:
eepurl.com/cs8taP